The
Worry
Box

Marion Halligan was born in Newcastle on the east coast of Australia and grew up by the sea. She has spent several years intermittently in France and now lives in Canberra with her husband and occasionally two children.

Author of three novels and three collections of short stories, she has been nominated for most of the major literary prizes. Her book *The Living Hothouse* won the 1989 Steele Rudd Award for the best collection of short stories and the Braille Book of the Year, and *Eat My Words* received the Prize for Gastronomic Writing in 1991. She was also winner of the 1990 Geraldine Pascall Prize for book reviewing and criticism.

Marion Halligan has published over sixty stories in magazines and anthologies in Australia and overseas, as well as articles and conference papers on food.

The Worry Box

Marion Halligan

MINERVA

Published 1993 by Minerva
a part of Reed Books Australia
22 Salmon Street, Port Melbourne, Victoria 3207
a division of Reed International Books Australia Pty Limited

Reprinted 1993

Typeset in 10/14 Berkeley by Midland Typesetters, Maryborough, Victoria
Printed and bound in Australia by Australian Print Group

National Library of Australia
cataloguing-in-publication data:

Halligan, Marion, 1940- .

The worry box.

ISBN 1 86330 238 7.

A823.3

For James-Sebastian

Contents

Contents

Previous publication

The Worry Box: *Phoenix*. The Circus: *Penthouse*. The Ambient Carriage: *Fine Line*. Caravan: ABC Radio National. The Orangery: *Descant*. Cafe Society: *Southerly*.

Cherubs: *Australian Short Stories*. Oysters: *Antipodes*. Multitudinous Teas Incarnadine: *Westerly*. Death and the Mother: *Southerly*. Decay: *Meanjin*. Beneficiaries: *Meanjin*, ABC Radio National, *Paris Transcontinental*. Salut, Dr Appleton: *Southerly*. Vale, Professor Appleton: *Voices*.

Mirror Man: *Uneasy Truces* (Penguin). I Love You: *Kunapipi*. Tale Telling: *Kunapipi*. The Power of Words: *Westerly*. Tryst: *Overland*. Neighbourhood Fortress: *Crimes of a Summer Christmas* (Allen & Unwin). The Ice-cream Bursts: *Crimes of a Summer Christmas 2*. Induction: *Westerly*.

Acknowledgements

I am most grateful to the Literature Board of the Australia Council for the support and encouragement they have given me over the years; their interest has played an important role in my writing.

My thanks also to Seven Writers, who helped me learn to read my own work.

part one

◆ ❖ ◆

*S*tories

of

Unease

The
Worry
Box

*T*he house is full of bad dreams. They lurk in the curtains like ugly smells, they infest the carpets like the dust mites that may kill babies in their cots. Shake the curtains, beat the carpets: the dreams are tenacious, they cannot be dislodged. They hatch, they multiply.

Consider then the process of disinfection.

This can be done by the burning of sulphur, at the rate of one pound to every thousand cubic feet. The sulphur is best set alight in an iron dish supported upon a basin of water. The room must be sealed tightly, the windows and chimneys pasted over with brown paper, and the fumes allowed to remain for twenty-four hours. Afterwards the place should be ventilated for a week. Alas, the sulphur injures fabrics and paintings, and bleaches colours. Does this mean that the dreams will no longer be in technicolour? And where's the benefit, for black and white is just as powerful.

Sulphur can also be taken orally, then it's called flowers of sulphur, and mixed with treacle, administered every Saturday morning regular as a Victorian childhood, not nice but excellent for cleansing the system. Maybe of bad dreams too.

Perhaps it will be better to call in the ridder of dreams. Listen for his plaintive cry in the streets as he goes his rounds, ready to ply his trade. Dreams rid, dreams rid, he sings. Long calling has twisted the words out of their shapes into a chant. It is like the cry of the knife grinder; you understand it not because you can decipher it but because you know what it is. Up and down the streets he goes, crying dreams rid, dreams rid—you believe—and people run out and invite him in. Even if you do not want him that day his melancholy musical call is a comfort; next time you can have your knives sharpened, your pianos tuned, your dreams eliminated.

In this house the dreams are everywhere. Upstairs with the parents. Downstairs with the children. In the blue room with the guests. Even the cats mutter and twitch in their myriad sleeping places. At breakfast people meet. I had a curious dream, they say. Or strange. Frightful. Fearful. Horrible. Sometimes they tell one another what they were, other times they say they can't remember. At this, people wonder whether they really can't remember, or whether it is that the dreams are too terrible to relate.

This is one of the dreams. A woman and a man fall in love, suddenly, direly. They can't touch, it's always too public, they can only look. They make love with their eyes. They walk along the street like two old friends out for a stroll, pottering, hands behind backs, looking down at their feet that move so tidily across the ground. Imagine I am kissing you, she murmurs; all the way along the street she speaks to him and he to her of the intimate physical facts of their lovemaking; they never touch, except in these words. It's exquisite blissful misery, emotion so intense, such desire, such longing, such absence, such pain, that they are almost perfectly happy. Their pleasure dazzles them. They stop at the street corner. She holds out her nightgown which is patterned with small black daisies. It's the same as yours, she says, spreading the folds of the gown her companion is wearing, and looks up into the face of her lover's wife.

There are dreams of sex that leave the vagina aching and wet and ashamed. They come from the incubus that lies on top of the sleeper, copulating, suffocating. The incubus has gleaming reddish eyes and in the mirror it isn't there. The long lying breathless warmth of the incubus incubates . . . the house is full of its hatchings.

The house at night is a Pandora's box inhabited by the creatures of malice, envy, spite; of rheumatism, colic, gout; of lust and melancholy. They seethe and whisper and prick and sting. But where is Pandora? Not there lifting the lid. The whole turbulent malaise stays shut inside, the house dwellers with it.

One day the woman dreams that she calls in the ridder and he refuses to come. She hears his cry in the street and runs out to him. Courteously he follows her, but when they get to the door of her house and she opens it, her gestures inviting him in, he draws back, his arm across his forehead and his head bowed as though expecting blows. I cannot come in, he says. What's to be done, if even the ridder of dreams is defeated? She wakes up and thinks, at least it was only a dream.

The daughter dreams of a huge ugly old woman who passes her in the street. I will put that child in my pocket, says the crone, her skinny finger pointing. When the girl wakes up she is dead.

The man dreams of his father, who has just died. Often

he dreams that he's still alive. He tells his wife, who comforts him. One night the father comes and says, I've been ill, but I'm much better now; there was no need to give up hope. The man is overjoyed, and then embarrassed. He has taken the father's things, sold some, used some for himself, terrible mistakes have been made. The father smiles. It doesn't matter, he says.

That's Jung's dream, the guest tells them at breakfast. Jung had exactly that same dream. He says it's archetypal.

The guest dreams that she is a child playing with her sister in a deserted rubbish dump. It's full of desirable things, a piano shivered out of shape by its fall, a tall typewriter with keys like lily-pads, a yellow pumpkin vine whose flowers they wear as hats. They find a packet of sugar cones, they think of ice-cream, prickly with crystals, and there is a refrigerator. It's a Silent Knight, with a silver helmeted head on the front. This noble head will save them from the ghosts in the typewriter. The children climb in and the door slams shut. It's perfectly dark. They scratch one another, they claw and fight, struggling to get out. The door won't yield but the flesh does. They scream and cry, tearing at each other, drawing blood, weeping, then there is silence and a great weight on the chest. The woman cannot move for the great heated squatting weight on her chest, depriving her of breath. In the morning she rings her husband and waits for him to tell her their children are all right.

The guest listens for the cry of the dream ridder. She is afraid to leave, in case the dreamings go with her. She wants to make sure she sloughs them off before she goes, discarding them like the cobweb skin of a lizard found under the kitchen cabinet by a young girl and pressed for safe-keeping in a bible.

The daughter tries to stay awake, for sleep puts her in the old woman's pocket, where there is no air, no light, only the poison of mothballs and dirty lint that winds about her like a snake. And when she wakes up she will be dead.

The father dreams again about his father. Brothers and sisters are cleaning out the family house, it's practically empty, only remains the stuff they don't know what to do with, decent things, valued once, not proper to be given to St Vinny's or the Smith Family, but nobody wants them. Their father is there, observing them. Father . . . you're here, you're all right . . . I'm still dead, says the father. Just come to see how you're getting along. The son is ashamed, the old family house is a box, divided into boxes, the ceilings tall, the spaces echoing with emptiness. How can they be forgiven for turning their father's house into a box? For taking his things, and worse, not taking them. The old man looks around. The judgement is all in the son's fear of it. Thought I'd come and have a look, the old man says, and that's what he's doing. Observing. Like a child, without passion. The son suddenly realises: What's it like, Dad, there. The father thinks. Cups of tea, he says. When the son wakes up that's all he can remember: cups of tea. And that he wanted to ask about his mother, was Dad there with her, and couldn't quite bring himself to, being afraid of the answer. Cups of tea, he tells his wife. That's all I found out about life after death.

His wife doesn't tell him her dream, of silver figures in a cupboard, malleable, unspeakable. They are instead of people, they replace people. Handy in a cupboard. They are part of a large network of soul-stealing, body-stealing. Of an immensity ungraspable. They shine in the dark cupboard. Malleable and obscene.

The old lady in whose pocket the daughter is wound in snaky lint chinks and clatters china. They make a good cup of tea here, she says. They scour their teapots. A voice replies, Ah, it's the sign of a good place if they scour their teapots.

7

The next day the daughter asks, Mummy, do we scour our teapots? Not really, we just rinse them. Why?

Among the books the man keeps from his father's library is *The Best Dramatic Poems*, cost one and thruppence, for learning and reciting at parties and other sociable gatherings, so you are not one of those people who don't object to being entertained but refuse to do their share of the entertainment. A poem you could learn is 'The Picture of Ginevra', a version of the oak chest story. Lovely Ginevra, prized by her father since her mother died of the gift she gave, is married in her fifteenth year to her childhood playmate and first love, but come the bridal feast, she has disappeared. Never to be found. The husband flings away his life in battle with the Turk, the father wanders in mind and body, looking for—he knows not what. Fifty years pass, some young people shift an old mouldering chest, it falls apart, and there's a skeleton . . .

> *With here and there a pearl, an emerald stone*
> *A golden clasp, clasping a shred of gold,*
> *All else had perished, save a nuptial ring*
> *And a small seal, her mother's legacy,*
> *Engraven with a name, the name of both,*
> *'Ginevra'.*

Good stuff for reciting at parties, this. Good nightmare stuff. Lying in the chest. Can't lift the lid. Pushes, but no leverage. Hears voices, running, shouts. Beats with her fists, her satin-shod feet. Calls, screams, yells. No one hears, no one stops. Running feet, drumming, thudding. Flickering torches. How does she know? The light comes through a hole as big as a nail in the lid. They are there and do not hear her. They pass and it is dark again. There is a hole in the lid, she will not suffocate. She is buried alive and will not suffocate.

This is the nightmare, the monster that sits on the chest and presses, crushes, the *cauchemar* that oppresses, against whom the sleeper struggles in vain. The nightmare heavy as the burial chest suffocates the speaker with dreams of not suffocating.

A guest comes to stay and brings a present. It's a small box, from Guatemala, half as big as an eggcup, made of split wood thin as a shaving, painted with a brief bright pattern. Inside are eight tiny figures, wrapped in coloured wool and fabrics that make trousers, skirts, sombreros. They are worry people, this is a Guatamalan worry box. You put them under your pillow and they worry for you. So you can sleep unharmed.

The woman puts the box under her pillow and sleeps. In the morning the box is crushed and all the little people are twisted and contorted, some have lost their heads. She realises that the house she lives in is a worry box, dwelt in by people expert at worrying, real professionals, and a lot tougher than the tiny Guatamalan people. The only question is, whose pillow is it under?

The
Circus

*T*his story happened in the sort of time that has once put upon it, but it is not therefore particularly old. If you look carefully you might see a touch of art deco in its trimmings, though that may be imagination. And it occurred in a country where time behaves differently from here.

There and then lived a couple, a man and a woman, peasants perhaps you could call them, or farmers. They worked hard and lived well. When they killed a pig they made black puddings from the blood, white from the flesh, and sausages from the intestines, they stewed the ears and grilled the feet, smoked the hams and roasted the forequarters, fried potatoes in the fat, made cheese from the head and bacon from the ribs, potted the liver and fricasseed the brains. They grew grain for bread, and milked cows and goats for cheese. Grapes swelled and were crushed into wine, and the virgin oil was pressed from the olive.

Hard work, good living. The blade turning the soil, the knife at the pig's throat, the shears on the sheep's back, all were steps in the processes that brought fruition. The windfall apples for jelly, the mushrooms in the woods, the berries on the canes and the nuts on the trees—all were to be depended on, they did not fail.

The man and his wife were short people, with abundant flesh firmed by toil. The woman was round; she looked as though she could have been modelled by a child in a series of spheres, the child with tongue tipped between teeth carefully rolling different sized balls between her palms, the head and its two apple cheeks, the breasts, the buttocks, the stomach; even the arms more spherical than not. Whereas the husband resembled a set of cubes, a box of a body, and neck and shoulders and muscular arms all squared. Their skins were strong and pale brown, russet-coloured where the sun had caught them, and they had straight dark hair that shone when certain lights fell upon it. At night they lay in lavender linen, tired with the proud contented tiredness of work well done, and took pleasure in one another.

It's a golden age picture, but it has a flaw—and that a classical one. They had no children. It was difficult in a life devoted to fruitfulness to be barren. The woman's spherical hips seemed made to house a child. They hoped, they prayed, they did all the practical things, without success. In their middle age, when they had accepted that their role was to succour fecundity and not to enjoy it, they were surprised to discover themselves pregnant.

A boy was born, a beautiful child. From the beginning he was pale, never having the boiled look of most babies. He was delicately made, too; if his mother was spherical and his father cubic, then he was linear. Even as a baby, he was not plump;

his arms and legs, his fingers and toes, were long and slender, and his jaw, his lips, the almonds of his eyes were fine curving lines. There was no suggestion that he was not perfectly strong, absolutely healthy, and indeed he never suffered the usual childish malaises, but his mother looked after him as a precious and fragile creature needing care. And a little mysterious. Sometimes when she lay him on the bed to change his nappy, the expression on her face was that of the Virgin Mary regarding the Christ Child. Not that she treated him with awe. She kissed his tummy and nibbled his toes and rolled him in somersaults when he wriggled and kicked. And when in the manner of little boys lying nappyless on their backs his penis stiffened and he peed in a yellow arc on the front of her dress, she laughed and picked him up and cuddled him and blew in his neck. Neither the mother nor the father could any more remember or even imagine what their lives had been like without him.

One evening when he was about three they were all sitting around the fire. The mother was knitting and the child was playing with the things his father brought him—a pine cone, a stone from the river, the polished skull of a fox—or made for him, as now, carving wood into sensuous shapes. As the woman knitted she looked at them, at the man and his rosy brown squareness, at the slender fair child, at her own stubby brown fingers plying the wool. Perhaps he's a changeling, she thought. There'd been gipsies down by the river the night that he was born. The midwife had asked for silver to cross their palms; better to buy a blessing than risk a curse. Perhaps there had been an exchange, perhaps the beautiful boy on the hearthrug was really a little prince, son of a noble house. This was a warm, well-fed, happy-family-safe-by-the-fire fantastical thought. Not for a moment did she doubt the child was hers.

His miraculous beauty was a gift to his parents, and a gift from them.

By the time that he was five it was clear that he was quick as well. The priest noticed the way he looked at words and offered to educate him. He taught him to read, and gave him some lessons in mathematics and grammar, but he was old and sleepy and often the boy roamed his library and educated himself, oddly and passionately. The old man had conversations with him, and wondered if he learned more than he taught. He saw that the child as he grew towards youth looked like an angel in a medieval painting, with fine-limned face smiling upon a lute or harp. He didn't say so to anybody; nobody would have known what he meant.

Although the parents had wanted a child out of some apprehension of survival, of continuance in life as well as after it, they didn't see him as a peasant or a farmer. He was too delicately made for hard work; he was quite strong but had not the stamina. He kept busy about the place, but did not toil as his parents did. He set out the cheeses on vine leaves, wrote labels for the jars of preserves, collected the eggs, searched out mushrooms. And talked to them. He was a great entertainment.

This was a very good life, for all three, and nobody imagined that it might not go on. When the boy was thirteen two things happened. They were not connected, but their joint occurrence made it difficult not to see causation. The child grew breasts. His mother noticed it during the summer. He was wearing a white linen shirt, and when he stretched up to pick cherries the falling of the light and the blowing of the wind made it impossible to mistake; they were youthful, but definitely formed, small pointed lumps upon the tight cage of his ribs, and the nipples standing out. At that moment a weight fell upon the mother, as it never had before, even in all the childless years, a weight like a great woollen blanket seamed with lead. It bowed her shoulders and made breathing difficult. Sometimes briefly she forgot it was there but always its heaviness recalled its presence. She watched the child; he seemed as serene as ever. Sitting in the kitchen, herself knitting, her husband snoozing, she looked at his head bent over a book. It occurred to her that perhaps he'd always known, that all the years of his childhood, when all his physical features were those of a boy, he'd felt within himself female as well as male. Inside her head she put words together, lumpy spiky words that fell far short of her intention. She'd never had much time for talk; she'd touch, she'd smile, she'd sing, people understood her. The child said enough for them all. Now she sat with her knitting, casting round for words and their connections to make a net to catch the meaning of this situation, and failed.

The other thing that happened during the winter was that her husband, an old man now, had a stroke. Not a very bad one but it slowed him down.

The heavy clothes of winter disguised the child's shape, but when the summer came it was evident. His breasts had grown; drastically they changed the shape of his summer shirts. Though he stayed at home, word got around. His mother knew from the way eyes followed her at the market, the murmured words behind sidelong glances. The priest came to the house. The mother thought, he's come to see for himself, he's come to inspect. What he said was: Whatever's happened to your lessons, child? I've missed them.

The youth smiled. Thanks to them I know the name for myself. Hermaphrodite. The word came out of his mouth like an almond tree bursting into flower. Named after Hermes, the messenger of the gods, who presides over commerce and thievery, who invented the lyre, and Aphrodite, the goddess of love. I think I have to finish lessons now. My parents need me.

The father could no longer work hard. The youth and the woman did their best, but his slenderness and delicacy were exacerbated by his femaleness; she was like a sapling, tough and strong but pliant and easily bowed; she lacked the power to work as her father had done. A pig was not killed; half the grapes rotted on the vines, sometimes the milk curdled before the cheese was made. As the hard work became difficult the good life slid away. It was hard not to see the child's change as the beginning of the draining away of the good things.

The husbandry of the past sustained them for a while. They were not near starvation, though a winter might come when there was no more food. Jars of quince and rowanberry and blackcurrant preserves still glittered on the dresser, the wings and legs of geese and ducks still nestled in their own dense white fat, olives swam in oil, but the shelves were no longer full; use exceeded replenishment.

In the autumn of the child's fifteenth year, when his body had all the shapes of its adult frame but still belonged to a child, as though the flesh were dressing up, were playing at maturity, a man came to the house. He was a big man, thickly blackly haired, and when he smiled the skin inside his mouth glistened red. He offered a lot of money.

For the kid. The boy–girl. Or is it girl-boy? Oh, the fame has spread, don't worry. He—she—it—whatever!—could make you rich, you know.

He smiled. The red flesh glistened.

Oh no. No, said the woman. He's not for sale.

Who's talking about selling? I'm talking about a job. A career. Easiest job in the world. Lap of luxury. And an excellent income, no effort.

I don't understand what you mean.

Look, I run a show . . .

A freak show, said the youth.

Not at all, not at all. The man looked hurt. He pouted red skin too. This is a class act. Talented artistes. Unique specimens. Travel to some of the finest venues in the world. It's easy living, all right. Nothing to do but lie on a silken couch and smile— all the way to the bank.

No, said the mother, and the father.

I'll make you an offer you can't refuse. He took out more money than they'd ever seen before. Look, this down, and after that it's up to the kid, what it sends you every month. I pay a good wage. Of course there's keep and travelling expenses, but you'll find that there's a goodly sum left over.

No, said the parents, and whatever the swarthy man said they just kept saying no. They shook their heads to keep his words from their ears; they had no arguments to counter him, only stubbornness. Their child listened.

When the man left he said, I think I should go.

Are you mad?

It would be all right. A job. I could stop if I didn't like it.

You don't know. You don't know what it would be like.

When they'd gone to bed he went out. He wrapped himself in a cape that joined him to the darkness of the night and walked around until he found the man, in a cafe doored and windowed with yellow squares of light. He waited till he came out, and said, Give me the money and I will come and work for you. He wrote a note to his parents. I will see you again soon, was one of the things it said. They would have to get the priest to read it to them.

❖   ❖   ❖

The swarthy man had partly told the truth. The job was not hard physical work. Even the favours he had not mentioned as part of the deal were of a passive nature. There was no salary or wage, and the luxury was theatrical, a matter of persuading the imaginations of the customers. The players knew how frayed and stained it was. Players was said with irony. My players, the man sneered. They were all freaks. There was a dwarf, who was very strong; he did the manual work of the troupe—another sneer. There was a girl with a beard which was long, dark brown, very silky. It took up most of her time, in the conditions in which they travelled, washing it, putting it in curl papers, perfuming it. She never spoke, and nobody knew whether she could. She poked with her elbows and grabbed for food. There was a fat woman who spent most of her time in a sort of cart, or litter, reinforced with solid wooden beams in order to support her weight. She wouldn't wash. The others retched when they had to go near her. She didn't take any notice. It's all part of the experience I offer, she said. When they had to wait on her they held their breaths. There were hierarchies in the troupe, but no one member perceived them clearly. When the swarthy man said, Take her food, they did, holding their hands across their faces and gulping little puffs of air untasted down their throats.

The other member of the troupe was a two-headed sheep.

The maestro gave his newest acquisition a name. Stars always change their names, he said, and cackled with laughter. Hero, he said, we'll call you Hero. When its recipient pointed out that it was a girl's name he scoffed. A hero's always a man, he said. The name may have lacked ambivalence, the billing didn't. He's a Lovely Woman, it said. She's a Handsome Boy. When the maestro shouted his wares he played the pronouns for all they were worth. See him do her thing, he shouted. Is

he a her, is she a him. Come and see for yourself. Seeing him
do her thing, or seeing her do his thing, was a trick to get
the customers in. All Hero did was lie on a bench—the silken
couch, which was a wooden plank covered with a piece of
ancient grimy turquoise-coloured satin, with a tinselled tatty
pillow to put under his armpit or elbow—with a piece of gauze
over him. The maestro didn't want to make it too easy for people
to get value for their money. His only movement was into a
more comfortable position. He liked being called Hero. She could
be the beautiful girl waiting in the torch-lit tower for her lover
to come, or he could be the boy, the real hero, swimming the
stormy sea and finally perishing. Sometimes it was cold, but
usually heavy breaths and heaving bodies raised the temperature.
The bearded woman who was known as Barbara had to stand
up. She had a large palm leaf fan which she held over her
face so that she appeared an ordinary naked woman. Then
she moved the fan up and away from her in an arc, revealing
the shining curling beard, then back down again to hide it.
Up two three four five, pause; down two three four five, pause.
The latter pause the longer. The maestro believed in teasing.
The dwarf shared a booth with the two-headed sheep, and
mainly flexed his muscles. The sheep found simple existence
so fraught with warring choices that he usually did nothing.

The fat woman lay in her cart filling her booth with her
smell. The customers gagged and pulled out their handkerchiefs,
but quite enjoyed it. They were there to be appalled. She was
naked too, so there could be no suspicions of padding. She
picked up the great loops and pouches and pendules of her
flesh like a dancer holding out a frilled skirt, and watched the
watchers' faces. She was the only one who did this. All the
others had dead eyes. It was as though their bodies were on
show but their spirits were absent. So much so that customers

might accuse the maestro of using dummies, automata. If he were in a good mood he would bite the arm of Hero or Barbara and show the white teeth marks slowly fading, or prick them with a needle so that a drop of blood welled. Only the fat woman was present in her eyes, which had a challenging gleam. She took pleasure in displaying her grossness, as a means of taking revenge on their curiosity, punishing voyeurs by exceeding their expectations. She laughed at them when they looked sick at the sight and smell of her.

One day a customer hurrying out of her booth dropped a black silk scarf on the ground. Hero quick as a snake snatched it up and later cut slits in it so he could wear it as a mask. Sometimes he covered his eyes with it completely and lay on his couch with his mind as well as his eyes absent, thinking of the books he had read in the old priest's study, turning their pages again in his head. Sometimes he thought of his home, the vines in rows, the warm cow in the barn, the shifting silvery grey of the olive trees, his parents. These thoughts were dangerous, they turned sharp knives between his ribs. He would change position suddenly in order to get away from them, a bonus for the customers. He didn't often think about his present situation, though he wondered sometimes if he was disappointed. After a while he no longer knew whether he'd expected anything better. Sometimes he said the name for himself over in his head. Hermaphrodite. It had a beautiful shape, full of meaning. Hermaphrodite. And the fact that there was a name for him was a comfort.

Some of the old priest's books had had pictures, and one day reclining with his eyes glazed over he felt like one of them. He was lying with his knee bent up and his arm across it; something in the way his finger pointed transported him into the painting. He was Adam being given life; no, not just Adam,

Adam and Eve. Both at once: Adameve, Evadam: as good a name as hermaphrodite. His mind played with the idea, then bits of doggerel came into it. His lips smiled.

> *Adam and Eve and Pinch Me*
> *Went down to the river to bathe*
> *Adam and Eve were drowned . . .*

He became aware of something prodding his genitals. His eyes unglazed and he saw a woman with a face like a pudding, her hat the basin. She held out a walking stick with which she was poking at his penis, lifting it with a grim fraud-expectant look. Beside her two girls tittered behind their hands.

He grabbed the stick and twisted it out of her hands, hissing, Who do you think was saved? The woman reached out for her stick; Hero swished it through the air like a cane. His strokes whipped the shape of her body, her face, her shoulders, her legs. She could not get near it. She looked at the girls; Hero shaped them with swishings of the stick. All three drew back and went uncertainly out of the tent, looking over their shoulders as though everything might change and the cane acquiesce to their grasp. Hero kept the stick and used it as a prop. Sometimes, reclining on one elbow, he flexed it between his hands. The maestro was delighted. Kinky, he said. Kiinnkyy. I love it.

❖   ❖   ❖

The maestro's failure to pay a wage didn't matter because he regularly drank himself into unconsciousness and then Hero helped himself. He could do this because he was his bedfellow. Barbara had been ousted by him; she glowered and though he tried to win her would not be friends. She sat in front of the mirror staring at herself with large panicked eyes; she would examine her beard closely, looking for grey hairs, pluck them out with fury and then not want to throw them away. She smoothed the skin beside her eyes with anxious fingers against wrinkles. Hero shared the money with her, which enraged her, since before she'd kept it all, and with the dwarf and the fat woman, which enraged them because they'd realised they'd been missing out. There wasn't a lot of it, the troupe not being a great money earner, and some had to be left with the maestro for expenses, and to prevent suspicion. Hero made a pocket in the black silk scarf and always wore it; the others constantly accused one another of stealing. He wished they could be friends; they all had problems, a bit of kindness, a bit of affection, would make them easier to bear.

Speak for yourself, dearie, cackled the fat woman. Look after number one, that's my motto.

Only a fool trusts fools, growled the dwarf.

Barbara sneered.

The troupe travelled around in two clumsy wooden vans. The maestro drove one, the dwarf the other. The maestro's housed Hero, with Barbara in an alcove behind, and valuable goods like the turquoise satin and the tinsel pillow; the other carried the fat woman, and the booths, and the sheep in a pen hung on the back. Hero looked out of the window at the world jogging by, at cathedrals and castles and cities, and rivers flowing under bridges, and at fields and farms and trellising vines, though sometimes he had to look away from these because of the knives between his ribs. The maestro would stop the caravans in fields on the edges of towns, or on patches of waste ground in the middle of cities, and he and the dwarf set up the booths, flimsy partitions of wood and canvas, covered with faded painted signs like magic spells. Sometimes he'd attach them to a fair, or a circus, and then Hero would listen to the melancholy roars of animals he knew by name but not by sight. On such occasions the maestro kept them locked up so people couldn't catch free glimpses of his wares. At show time he put on his top hat and purple frock coat and spruiked; customers with fearful fascinated faces would hand him coins and file past the exhibits. In between spruiking—See the fat lady, 33 stones if she's an ounce, ladies and gentlemen, I've known smaller elephants, if she stands on you you'll wish it was an elephant—he hurried them along, on the grounds that they were depriving other people of these truly astonishing sights, but hoping that they'd pay again and go through for a second look.

In one city—they came to it across a river so wide Hero wondered if it might have been the Hellespont—he arranged a private show. A number of men sat on benches round one of the booths, the turquoise satin was spread in the middle, and a lot of money was taken. The maestro brought in Barbara and Hero. There was to be a special act between them. He played pander. He pushed them together, he took their hands and put them on the other's private parts, he cajoled, he murmured in the tone of endearments the things they were to do to one another. The seated men guffawed, they shouted encouragement as though it were a cockfight, they called out lewd asides and nudged elbows. The two performers faced one another. Their bodies were as dead as their eyes. They were like automata whose clockwork has run down; they couldn't perform. The audience began to swear, to make catcalls, to throw clods. The un-lovers stood wooden and undefended. The maestro cursed them, threatened them, softly, smiling, but could not animate them.

In the end he had not just to give the clients their money back but buy them spirits. He nearly beat the two of them that time, coming back drunk and late to the caravan, but Hero said, Remember our skins, which always stopped him. He was never so drunk as to damage his wares. It occurred to Hero that customers might be titillated by marks of the horsewhip in their flesh. He hoped it wouldn't occur to the maestro who, after the failure of the copulation, fed them water and pig bread for several days because he said he'd lost so much money over their stupidity.

The maestro was violent and they were all scared of him, except perhaps the fat woman who could shout more obscenities at him than he could reply to. After a while Hero realised that he wasn't vicious, nor particularly unkind; not a very bad man considering his trade. He was learning not to mind being his bedfellow; it was a warm place to sleep and often the maestro was too drunk to bother him. He never seemed to expect much response, was often content with holding, and Hero could go away into his own head, and think of Aphrodite with her swans and doves and shells, her clumsy husband and war-mongering lover, of Hermes in his winged cap and sandals flitting busily about the heavens, putting his skill and dexterity to good and bad purposes.

The bedfellow could also borrow the keys, and let himself out of the caravan. Provided he guessed right how long the maestro would sleep, he could have some hours of freedom. Hero stole one of Barbara's dresses and wore that; it was easier to disguise the male parts than the female ones. His hair had grown quite long, it curled over his shoulders. In the crowded city streets men cupped their hands round her bottom, pinched at her nipples; their bodies wreathed round hers. She was learning to slip out of their clutches with skill and dexterity. It hurt her to realise that she couldn't ever escape the lust of others; if their eyes did not pry at her, their hands did. Only in the dawns was she free, when the world was not yet occupied by people.

Occasionally the maestro had an odd customer, a man, better dressed and more fastidious than the usual crowd. Several times such a man came afterwards to the caravan, and offered the maestro sums of money for the hermaphrodite. As the maestro refused he would offer more; immense amounts were mentioned. Hero overhead one of these, and was surprised; such money would never be made from the booth. He understood that the man wanted to buy him to keep for himself, much as he would buy a fine bronze sculpture or a painting that pleased him. He heard him call him 'the catamite' which angered him, and was glad of the maestro's refusal, though the life would have been one of great luxury. At least in the booth he earned his living.

He's not for sale, the maestro said. His parents had said the same thing. In the same proud repelling voice.

❖   ❖   ❖

The maestro and his unique specimens arrived at the capital of a country in time for the spring fair. There were displays of skill in horse-riding and bull-baiting, exhibitions of an agricultural nature, and a series of booths like the maestro's displaying fire spitters, sword swallowers, glass eaters, nail sitters, knife throwers, fortune tellers, snake charmers, escape artists, who wandered the world as he did. They formed a large circle, known as Sideshow Alley, and in the centre was a circus, called The Prodigious Infants. They had a Big Top which was pink and white and looked like a sky-high iced birthday cake; the flags fluttering from its scalloped roof could have been candles flickering.

The maestro exhibited his wares all day and in the evening went out drinking with his fellow entrepreneurs. First he locked his people in. Hero had a copy of the key, and let them out.

The fat lady never moved if she could help it, but the dwarf and Barbara slipped off. Hero had discovered some of his clothes missing, and guessed that Barbara had stolen them for the same purpose as he had hers. He was wearing her dress and the heavy dark cape with a hood. Inside its frame her face was held like a drawing which glowed in the fairground lights; people's eyes were drawn to her. She went to the circus.

The Prodigious Infants were not all children; some were hardly more than babies but there were teenagers and adults as well. They specialised in trapeze acts, four or five people swinging through the air and catching one another just when it seemed impossible. The audience was either holding its breath or sucking it in, or sighing it out. In the silences between cymbals and drums the high fliers orchestrated a tentful of breaths.

Everything the circus performers did was patterned and complex. They made fans, a dozen people standing on the back of one strong man, hands linked, perfectly balanced. They made human chains that dangled from the heaviest to the lightest, and human columns that grew up in the same way. They formed a kind of hedgehog of people on a unicycle; she counted sixteen, standing on one another's shoulders, clasping hands, except for the outside people who held their free hands out in triumphant balance. Pink and white girls pirouetted on horseback in between turning somersaults in one another's arms. They smiled, they laughed, they were delighted with themselves. Their excitement welled out. But always with care, with control, so that their bodies had a kind of tension that responded to the needs of others. They vibrated, in unison or in patterns, like strings producing music, complex and moving harmonies. So that three trapeze artists could launch into the air at the same time, sure that the necessary hands or feet or swing would be in the precise place at precisely the necessary second. They flew out over the audience and trusted that what they needed would be provided. And it always was. The audience did not believe as the artists did; they kept expecting things to go wrong. That was where they got their excitement.

The circus finished with trumpets and triumphal marches. The performers laughed and waved, they couldn't even in tableaux keep still for a moment, their feet kept giving little trills of delight. When it was over Hero sat, exhausted with jealousy. The crowds left and the lights were extinguished, the tent grew cold, and she sat, jealous. It weighed her down, she couldn't move; despair froze worse than cold. She couldn't bear to think of the sneering troupe, passive and dead-eyed, exploiting and exploited. Hating. She would never go back.

The maestro found her. A grey morning revealed her slumped on a seat in the empty tent. He was in a rage, and grabbed her and shook her. Her body was lax, was limp with the jealousy and the despair and the cold; he had to hold her up to do it. I'll whip you, he babbled, I'll whip you, you'll wish you were dead. He had to carry her, her legs didn't work. Remember my skin, she muttered. He held her tight in his arms, and shook her. Her hood fell back, and her pale head, that there was nobody to recognise had the pure and heart-stopping lines of a medieval angel. He carried her home, hugging her tight in his arms. Never again, never, he mumbled, and pressed her to his chest. She felt his face wet against hers. His lips mumbled never never in kisses on her cheeks.

*Y*ou've been to the cinema, or
perhaps looked at movies on television. It's the nineteenth
century, cobbled streets, pointed houses, columns, perhaps,
narrow-staired lanes. And a carriage goes past. Slow. Anonymous.
The camera never following it. Briefly it looms, then leaves the
picture.

I'm the person in that carriage. Going to . . . Coming from . . .
You never find out.

The scene's not very brightly lit. In fact it's usually gloomy.
Possibly black and white, maybe becoming coloured as the story
proper begins. There are dim shots of the scene settings, the
shuttered houses, gutters running water, empty porticoes,
perhaps a fountain or a statue, even a dog, skinny starved mongrel
of a creature. There's a voice over, saying *It was the best of times,
it was the worst of times*, and my carriage comes trundling across.

27

Its wooden wheels grate on the cobbles, it pitches and rattles, the horse picks its way. The best of times. Ha.

Why not have an empty carriage, you ask. Just the man on the box and the interior vacant. That wouldn't do at all. My presence is needed. My felt life in that carriage is important to the verisimilitude. You may imagine you catch a white glance of arm, a pale head shape. Picture a lovely victim, a cold protagonist, not of course of this story but of all the others that are going on parallel and untold. If I am inside it is possible.

Sometimes you can barely see even the carriage because of the fog. You hear the wooden clopping of the horse's hooves, the muffled trundle of its wheels, maybe glimpse its faint bulk. It moves up Baker Street where a man in a complicated Victorian interior plays the violin. An imaginary man with a life of his own and believed to be real, so societies of people argue about the truth of his death, meeting all over the world to worry at the details of his life. And anonymous I in a carriage create an atmosphere for him to inhabit. In the yellow fog of coal smoke, now abolished, surfaces bead with a gritty moisture, and noises are squashed and sinister, in dirty-brick-housed Baker Street in the nineteenth century.

But the room is not there, not behind that streetscape, the room is in a quite other place, and should a carriage—never mine, mine is entirely a figment of the ambience—should a carriage stop outside and a man alight, or a woman heavily bonneted in the secretive style of visitors in these stories, and go up the steps and knock and be admitted, it will be to an opening in a facade. These characters will have to travel to a quite different place to find the complicated Victorian interior. May already have found it, may have conducted their business and been shown out, all in another day's shooting, and this scene of their arriving will be happening in fact after the event. Films don't care about chronology, there are only moments, uncausal as a pack of cards; here, shuffle us up a story.

Those glimpses you imagine you see of me, that pale arm, that indistinct globular shape that may be my piled-up weight of hair; remember Conrad and the woman with the weight of hair that so obsessed his narrating? Her little head, with shining coils of hair; her little face attractively overweighted by great coils of hair . . . That could be me. In a white shirt of soft stuff that loops in the sleeve and frills at the neck. All quite properly nineteenth century. But I trick you. Below I wear jeans. Become an improperly forked creature. And yet, the jeans are not so inappropriate as you might think. They are tight, they shape me, they require a certain straitness of posture. In other words, they demand that I assume a demeanour. Exactly as a corset does. So though my jeans are different in expression from a Victorian dress, they are essentially the same in nature, and thus apposite to the period. They may *be* another thing but they *do* the same. I am controlled for the sake of fashion. You can see it in the angle of my neck.

Did you notice the figure in jeans, just there, out of the corner of your eye, almost off the edge of the frame, ducking into a doorway of Baker Street? No? Well, you wouldn't have, I didn't do it, I only thought about it. You can imagine me, if you like, next time you see the ambient carriage, see it hesitate, and imagine a small anachronous androgyne flitting off to the left, not quite visible in the murk. After all, you are not obliged to take the camera's point of view. You could assert your autonomy.

I've said the scene is usually dim, but it doesn't have to be fog and yellow gloom; this is a sunny August day in Bond Street. *The Prince had always liked his London . . .* , and here he is strolling along observing on the one hand the shop windows that darkly frame the precious goods within and on the other the women's faces. My carriage isn't here, it isn't my scene at all. There are ladies in open vehicles; this is what the director is trying to achieve: *the tense silk of parasols held at perverse angles in waiting victorias*. He's not succeeding. Not a hope. It looks like Ascot Opening Day in *My Fair Lady*, all frill and fuss and flutter in time to the tinkling hopping tune of it, even the Prince in step, though the music is soundless. There's no tension in this silk, no perversity in the parasol angles. How could there be? The words are not susceptible of illustration, they would have been better left on the page for the reader to taste, to pick out and savour—enjoy it yourself, now—savour the *tense silk*, the *waiting victorias*. Not even the simpering ladies sitting in them know that these light low carriages with the collapsible hoods are named thus, after the then youthful queen still just reigning. So the Prince, in his pale pigskin gloves and his grey felt hat luminous as a pearl and surpassing exquisite, walks down a Bond Street as lacking in ambiguity as the shops in any dimension but the fronts you see here. How gracefully he strolls, but not subtly; thoughtfully we can see, but not of what. He's a good actor, but all we can see of his thoughts is their seriousness. A horse race, a marriage, a birthday present, a lost fortune, lunch; your guess is as good. Better to read the book and leave these scenes for simpler tales. Like . . .

With a twitch of his cane the Prince hails a passing hansom. Cut. Cut. Cut it out, cut it up. It's another fifteen pages before the cab will stop in Cadogan Place.

There, on cue, here I am, like John the Baptist going before, in my little closed carriage, two-wheeled, one-horsed, a pale blob of hair and shirt: did you see me? Probably you were noticing the hansom stopping, the prince alighting, turning, paying, pausing to fish out his watch on its chain, the hansom jogging away, the camera closing, his thumb on the knurled knob, the lid flying up, the face of the watch, its hands pointing to teatime.

In the meantime; ah, I've made use of my meantime. I've thumped on the roof with my umbrella and brought my brougham to a standstill beside the Prince. The camera can no longer see him. I open the door, beckon; he hesitates. This is not in the script. Is it? He glances back at the facade of the house in Cadogan Place. It stares blindly over his head. Quick, I say, hurry, and he gets in. Another thump with the umbrella and we are away, to the wooden clopping of the horse on the cobbles and the call of Cut! in the background, a mournful shriek like the cry of a blackbird.

He is very beautiful, this Prince, with his brown moustache and his dark blue eyes, far too beautiful for me. You need a billionaire daddy like Maggie's to buy him for you, and even then you have to pay with subtle skill for years to come, before you've earnt him. I could never afford a Prince like this. But I take his hand, he looks at me with his flower-dark eyes, his finger strokes my hair, my piled-up Conrad-weighty hair that sometimes slides down from its own heaviness. His pearl of a hat slips from his lap. I put up my face and give his bottom lip a little bite. His mouth opens to mine. This is the moment for the camera to retire, to pull out of the carriage, up to the knowing nodding coachman on the box, back from the dear old horse plodding away, off to one side to let it pass on and then standing still to follow it as it makes its way into the ever after, with its precious cargo of lovers at last united. Look at it jiggle with the force of their passion. Until it's a tiny dot in the distance, and up roll the credits.

James it ain't, but I'm enjoying it. There comes a time when you get sick of being part of the ambience, even though the money's good, when you've got to take your destiny in your own hands, become a heroine, even if only for a moment. Even if it's only in your mind's eye that the camera follows. Otherwise you could spend your life in an ambient carriage making atmospheres for others to inhabit. Singing *Someday da dee da dum* in a two-wheeled brougham jogging across the cobbles, while all the best stories are elsewhere.

Caravan

*P*eople said it was a gipsy caravan, though they could have known such a thing only from books. Perhaps they were remembering Mr Toad's canary-coloured cart, taking out a picture long stored in the mind. This one was not just yellow, it was emerald and blue as well, and carved wherever possible, with gilt trimmings. There were cutouts in the walls in the shape of fleurs-de-lys and trefoils, but those who supposed them to be peepholes were disappointed. Nor did the windows offer any glimpses of the insides, because they were painted too, with pink and white cherubs juggling golden balls. It was altogether a startling object, and people who saw it found themselves thinking about it for the rest of the day, and often for long afterwards.

Is it a circus caravan, children asked.

Not exactly, their parents replied.

The caravan belonged to five women. They were all tall with red frizzy hair. Their bodies were slim and they were long-armed; their hands and feet were narrow. They wore clothes as carved as the caravan, encasing their legs and arms, and necks, waists and backs, leaving the rest bare. Their breasts and buttocks were painted in brightly coloured patterns which those who had seen them said were wonderful works of art, so intricate and moving that the eye could lose itself in them. Their pubic hair, which was red too, red as gold, was plaited and knotted and decorated with ribbons and jewellery; dark glowing stones: garnet, chalcedony, lapis lazuli, and pale cabochon emeralds.

Anybody could see the caravan from outside. It might park anywhere: in wide-pavemented Forrest; in the parliamentary triangle; in middle-aged suburbs where government boxes are busy cape-codding; in the new wastelands where large houses squat on Spanish-arched five-car garages resembling service stations. People are not sure how it gets there. Romantics like to imagine it horse-drawn, but that seems unlikely. Certainly there is never any evidence, in the form of a small steaming pile, for nearby residents to scoop up and boast of its value in their pampered gardens. The caravan is there, one day, standing by the side of the road, and another, it isn't. Sometimes it stops by the lake, and couples gliding past on large leisurely-wheeled bicycles remark on the vividness of its colours. Like a gingerbread house, says one.

Some lucky people will get to send in lunches, but that's not given to everyone. An eminent satirist, who has asked not to be named, though it can be admitted that he plays varied roles and both sexes, was spending considerable time on the choosing of suitable dishes. Do you think they will be tired of lark pâté, he asked. So delicate their palates must be. One is afraid of offending, or at least of not pleasing.

Some people, but these are few, are rare, will see the show. Show. Show.

One day a girl knocked at the door of the caravan. Armandine opened it.

Will you take me with you, the girl asked. I would like to join you.

No, said Armandine. You are slender, but you are neither tall nor red enough.

Perhaps, if she grows, one day, said Lily, whose skin was as green as a snowdrop.

We are enough, said Armandine.

The girl who was insufficiently tall willed herself to grow, but she couldn't find the caravan again.

A politician remarked rather wistfully that he would like to offer them lunch, but nobody told him how. As nobody talked about the . . . show? the performance? the exhibition? though there was some mention of tumbling, when the patterns on breasts and buttocks became kaleidoscopic. So some people imagined.

Are they gipsies, a lunch-giver was asked. They are not from Egypt, he replied. Nor even Bohemia.

Eventually the caravan was sold, but it did not prosper under its new ownership. People stopped sending in lunches. It was abandoned one day, in the street where it was parked. It stood in the weather and the paint washed off. It became splintery grey wood, and the carvings and cutouts were clogged with dead leaves.

There was talk about what happened to the five women. A decade or so later it was noticed that in the better private schools there were a number of red-haired children, who were long-armed and strong, and that people did what they said.

The
Orangery

*T*his is a true story. And what's more, it really happened to me.

I was travelling on a train, northwards through France. It was a fast train, though it stopped sometimes. I'd brought several books with me, and had already finished one, and was well into the next. My companion was also reading, and we didn't talk much. Occasionally I'd stare out the window, but not often; the landscape flashed past so fast it didn't offer contemplation, just frustration at things missed before they were perceived. Occasionally I'd stare into the carriage, abstractedly, thinking about what I'd read.

The man sitting beside me had nothing to read, no book, no magazine, not even the trashiest of newspapers. I was thinking scornfully how boring it must be, how boring he must be, to sit the whole of this long journey with nothing to occupy his mind, when he spoke:

—You don't need to read in order to have your mind full, he said. There's a lot more going on in my head than any book could satisfy.

He was smiling and looking at me, so I assumed he was talking to me. I smiled too and went on reading.

The train slowed, and when I looked up it was pulling into a station.

—Come on, he said. I'll show you. And we can use our legs as well as our heads.

He saw my reluctance, and smiled, again. He had a sweet smile.

—The train will stop for a long time. At least ten minutes. It's timetabled.

I looked out the window and there were orange trees in tubs, covered with a mixture of fruits and flowers, and I was seduced by the idea of getting out of the closeted air-conditioned train and breathing the sharp scented air of the orange blossom, so I put my books on the seat and followed him.

—See what a beautiful station it is, he said, pointing upwards, where tall slender iron columns flowered into arches supporting a filigree of milky panes of glass. The place was filled with pearly light and warmth.

—The stationmaster has created an orangery here; look at it: so far north and out of season he grows not just oranges, but lemons, and cumquats, mandarins, tangerines, limes.

Much of the platform was taken up with terracotta tubs of these trees, shining with globes of fruit in all the colours of orange and yellow, and the air was heady with the almost unbearable beauty of the citrus blossoms' scents.

—There's a lot to dwell on there, he said. Get started thinking about orangeries and it could take you hours.

He put his fingers under my elbow.

—The stationmaster is happy for people to pick them, but he likes to be asked. Come on.

We began to walk along the platform, and my senses were pierced by the pleasures offered: the air, unexpectedly balmy against my skin, the shining globes of fruit delighting my eyes, the scent filling my nostrils. I imagined the taste of the flesh of an orange or perhaps a mandarin bursting in my mouth.

We came to the end of the train. We still hadn't found the stationmaster but the platform and the fruit trees stretched out before us.

—There should be music, I said. Harpsichords, don't you think, in an orangery? Recorders. Viola da gamba . . .

I heard another sound. The clank of carriage couplings. I turned round and saw the train pulling out. I began to run, with nightmare-heavy legs, hopelessly; the train very swiftly acquired its silent electrical speed. My acquaintance stood and watched me walk back to him; I couldn't think what else to do.

—You see, when you're not in a book, things happen.

—I'd rather read about unpleasant things than live them. This is a disaster. I could feel panic rising. Whatever shall we *do*?

—There's the stationmaster. We'll ask him to let us pick some fruit.

The stationmaster was wearing a braided uniform and standing in the high-domed foyer of the station; beyond him was the town square with people and cars busy in the thin winter sunshine. I was assembling the French for We've missed our train, what can we do? when there was a very loud noise, an explosion which made not just our ears but our whole bodies reverberate, so much that balance faltered and we staggered against one another. Some of the filigreed panes of glass broke, falling in tinkling shards around our heads; one scratched my face. When they hit the platform they broke again and sent splinters stinging against our legs. Black smoke poured into the square from somewhere to the right.

There was a great murmuring groan of human voices. *La Samaritaine*, it said. *La Samaritaine*.

My companion had grown very pale. What does it mean, I asked.

— *La Samaritaine*. The department store. Big. Full of shoppers. Christmas. A bomb. Terrorists.

He spoke slowly, as though by saying the words, the names of things, without syntax, he took the import full in his mind. Then, that done, he grabbed my hand and began to run.

— Come on. We have to help.

I didn't go with him. I pulled my hand away and let him run on without me. I was terrified of seeing people hurt. At home I turned my eyes away from such sights on the television.

I stood in the high-domed foyer of the railway station with my eyes tight shut and wanted not to see. Helpers began to bring some injured people into its warmth and shelter and to sit on the chairs or lie on the floor and I couldn't stay there, in the way, hearing them.

I thought I would go out of the station the other way, away from the bombing, and leave it to the authorities, the experts, the people who had training and talents for this sort of thing, to fix it up. I crossed the line and went out the other side—I think I did. Somewhere I found myself walking beside a smelly canal, past the dismal shuttered backs of stores and warehouses. My mind was milling with profitless thoughts, of where I might be—some decent-sized provincial town, obviously, but I couldn't work out which, and hadn't noticed a name amongst all the orange trees—and how I might continue my journey, thoughts so jumbled and muddled with terror at human nature wanting to harm its fellows, desiring hurt and so successfully, that I wasn't functioning as a sense-making creature at all.

I turned the corner of a tall building with windows painted grey and came across people—bodies—some on stretchers, some on the ground, some covered with blankets, some with blood. There were ambulances there, and people helping. A man shovelling up broken glass; there was a finger amongst it. All this I saw in the brief flash before closing my eyes and turning away. But I couldn't shut out the noises. I thought of that, how you can close your eyes but not your ears, you can't stop your ears from hearing no matter how strong the will is, as I retreated from this back-door of the bombing. I hurried away with my head down and my eyes lidded, leaving just a slit to watch where my feet went. I was lost, turning unknown corners, fleeing but not escaping, unable to lose the sound of sirens, the smell of burning, in wanderings senseless and circular. With my head full of useless thoughts, circular, senseless.

I was saved by a name that cast a spoke in these whirling thoughts, simply by being an organisation of letters that I recognised. Théophile Gautier was this name, God-loving Gautier, who knows if he was, written in low relief across the facade of a building. It was a school, the Ecole Théophile Gautier named after the poet, a building of red brick with white rustication, recalling those garden factories where workers used to make sweets in model conditions, and very like my primary school. I went up the white plastered steps, along the unpolished slightly furry familiar dusty wooden floor of the corridor, and into a classroom. On each desk was a pad of that French paper that voluptuously demands to be written on, paper dense and bluish-coloured, with vertical as well as horizontal lines marking it in a grid of slightly darker blue. Write on me, it says. Trace your inky lines across my surface. See what sense you make.

The china ink-wells were dry. I went to the press in the corner and took a large stone bottle of blue-black ink and, first emptying an ink-well of the little balls of blotting paper that had amused some school child's idle hours, I poured the redolent fluid in. There were pens in the press, a box of yellow-varnished wooden pens with steel post-office nibs. I sat down at a desk and when I found a pen that wrote to my satisfaction I made my confession. Every few words I had to dip my pen afresh in the ink; the blue flowed dark and pale like a pulse beating.

I set down what I had done that day. What I hadn't done. I mentioned the finger on the ground shovelled up with the rubbish. I described my failure. Not a failure of help. I doubt that I could have helped. I might have been able to comfort, perhaps, though the people I put such effort into not seeing and wished not to hear might have been beyond comfort. But none of that is the point. What I should have done is looked at them. People like me suffered. I should have looked at them. I owed them that.

On the voluptuous paper I wrote my failure, that I didn't look when I should have, and I wrote that it showed me a truth about myself that I shall always have difficulty in living with. I thought how self-centred confession is; all those Is. If not Is then mes and mys. Maybe that is a punishment, not being able to escape your Is. Not being able to close your Is, any more than your ears. Then I tore off the sheets I had written, my fingers taking pleasure in the rich dense texture, and folded them in half to make a firm packet for carrying. I could only just see in the chalk-dim schoolroom. The day was ending.

Outside I walked through the streets, still lost, as it got darker and no lights were lit in the town. I carried my paper tight in my hand, a pale shape that my eyes burrowing through the darkness could barely discern. My confession. It was a condemnation. Or maybe it was an exorcism. I thought of both and couldn't tell which. The paper seemed a weight, and flimsy.

After a long time following the invisible ribbon of a concrete path by its feel underfoot I came out into a square where the light of a moon showed the angular burnt-out pile of *La Samaritaine* to my right, and I knew the railway station had to be behind me.

This moon shone through the ribs of the conservatory roof and glittered the shards of its glass on the platform, but there were no longer any mandarins or lemons, tangerines or oranges, clementines or limes or cumquats; those glowing orbed fruits and the trees that flaunted them had disappeared. There was only grey moonlight on grey stone. Perhaps a faint sharp scent of citrus reminded that an orangery had flourished here; but then, perhaps the odour was a memory, not a ghost. A scent is not so simply ascertained as a sight, and even there you do not always recall whether it was seen or dreamt or imagined or remembered. I thought of the train, that warm well-lit well-ordered space proceeding safely on its tracks to its destination, to the lucid capital, Paris, and inside it my companion and my possessions, the books that had immersed me, my woollen coat, a bottle of wine to pour red into round gleaming glasses. Baggage, luggage, belongings. I looked down at my hands; they were empty. I searched along the platform, went through the domed foyer and peered out at the square. The paper containing my confession was nowhere to be found. But I could not so easily mislay my guilt. The nightmare might gallop away like the train out of sight, but the airless memory of its weight still sat on my chest.

Cafe
Society

*F*rances had to spend the day in Goulburn. She was driving through the town early in the morning when the red warning light in the dashboard came on. Stop. It turned out the water pump had burst and would take all day to fix; the garage would have to telephone Canberra and get one sent over on the train.

She walked along the main street, down one side, up the other, of this town where people like her stopped for a quick coffee, a pee: nice old buildings, pretty park, see the sculpture on the insurance building, the band rotunda, the post office tower. Then hurry off, on to Sydney, Brisbane, London, home to Canberra.

She found a bookshop, after long looking bought a book, and went in to the cafe usually stopped at, a big bright place with red and gold paint and mirrors, a bar with bottles so glamorous they might have been artificial, and take-away chips and hamburgers. Down one wall were booths, and in the middle, tables. It wasn't as hideous as the big ugly cafe she and Rob used to meet in, that gaudy barn with terrible coffee, safe from friends and enemies. The booths secret, they'd thought then, but perhaps no more so than these. Maybe that was how his wife had found out.

Now she was a wife sitting in a cafe remembering being a girl in love with another woman's husband, thinking about the girl who was perhaps even now with her husband, in a cafe or in a bed, bed in the daytime is a lovers' stratagem but a husband was what Stephen insisted he was and wanted to be; he just wasn't stopping being a lover too. You have to choose, she said, and he agreed. But didn't.

Frances ordered coffee and began to read her book. It didn't hold her. Her eyes were drawn to the people around. She walked along to the newsagent, bought a foolscap pad, back to the cafe, another coffee. Thinking of Rob saying, What are you writing? when she'd met him again, after fifteen years. She was a writer of promise once. Schoolteaching, marriage, children, her cooking business: writing got lost. Turned into scraps of paper with words on them.

She begins.

Some people sit in cafes in Paris and write . . . novels . . . stories . . . poems. Masterpieces . . . works of art . . . literature. Me, I sit in a cafe in Goulburn and write—

Words on a piece of paper.

The cafe is busy, people come in, eat, drink, leave. Some are eating steak (*well done; actually, I like it burnt*) with mashed potatoes and chips and piles of vegetables, served on big oval plates, with white bread and butter. What unconventional mysterious disorderly lives are suggested by such meals at half past ten in the morning?

I knew a man who ate every night in the same cafe, and the same meal: ham salad. It would've had no dressing—or maybe salad cream offered—just the usual vegetables including celery curls and beetroot out of a tin. Every night of the week he ate this meal. It was in the Niagara Cafe, a place of dark polished wood and permanent boxes of chocolates, and the yellow light of frosted glass shells along the walls.

I didn't understand this at the time, to be able to afford to eat out and not try different places or at least different meals, but now I see the comfort of it. A friend of mine married him. She should have known better. He was not a good person to marry. Maybe if she'd given him ham salad every night it would have worked.

There's comfort in this cafe. It would always be the same.

Other people are eating cake, oozing alcoholic chunks of Black Forest, or cheesy cream cakes. Mothers buy paper cups of chips for their children while they drink coffee, staring into the distance, not alone but solitary in the manner of mothers. The kids chatter but the mothers don't hear. Travellers eat sandwiches and milkshakes. There are whole families having treats travelling.

A gunman comes in, carrying a rifle, probably one of those that shoot kangaroos and roadsigns for sport. He rakes the room with it, pointing it at an angle, just above headheight where the mirrors are. All the patrons get under the tables, the cafe people crouch behind the counter. He rakes the room with the gun again, and this time pulls the trigger. The mirrors crack into crazy jigsaws, and the pieces fall out. Tinkling they fall on to the glass-topped tables, on to the seats, into the sugar, the chips, the Black Forest cake. Slowly the pieces fall, one after the other, tinkling. The mirror jigsaw is all undone. Imagine the difficulty, putting back together a fallen mirror jigsaw. Making

45

all the reflections stay still until the pieces are back in place.

Squatting under the table I can see the gunman's feet, in scuffed cowboy boots, very high-heeled, with an ornamental metal spur across the heel. Above them, tight dirty jeans. Who is he? What does he want? What can cause or come of shooting up a country town cafe on a Tuesday morning?

The angst of unemployment, of fading farms . . . The despair of love betrayed . . .

The whole thing is ill-conceived. Anybody can see that. Violence is too hard. The gunman sits at the table and orders tea and cinnamon toast. He takes his hat off and puts it on the bench beside him. When the tea comes he spoons sugar into his cup, a third of the cup is sugar, and stirs it hard; all the while he eats his toast.

The mirror's crazy jigsaw is restored. There is a sense of order, of the fitness of things, in a country town on a Tuesday morning. The gunman's mouth is ringed with buttery cinnamon. His life is shut away inside him.

The ceiling in this cafe is very high and full of fluorescent light tubes. People say they imitate daylight, but daylight is never so cruel. The harshest sunlight is closer to the wish fulfilment (wishful thinking) of faces than these fluorescent tubes whose light is a lugubrious weight on the people underneath.

The gunman takes his now guiltless baggage and leaves. His place is taken by two people in love. The girl is a bit punk, with fishnet stockings and winkle-pickers, short leather skirt and a hairstyle of black stubble and blonde spikes with an orange frizz across her forehead, but she's an imitation, she's clean and pretty and tidy, her eyes are doe-painted and her ears hung with feathers that float with the turning of her neck. The boy is an equally ersatz bikie, leather clad and tattooed, looking at the world in this girl with innocent greedy eyes.

They order a milkshake with two straws and drink one another with their close-up eyes while they suck at it. They put it down and kiss milky sweet lips together, he holds her chin in his hands, then strokes her neck. He slides his hand through her festoons of gilt chains, then turns it, twists it in the chains, pulling tighter. Her eyes swell, her mouth opens, her tongue fills it. She sinks against his shoulder.

The waitress clears away the paper milkshake cup, the empty coffee cup, pushes the sugar and salt and the dispenser of stiff paper napkins to their proper place at the end of the table, wipes it down. The bikie picks up his girl and carries her out, stopping to pay at the cash register. He stands with one foot on a chair, resting the girl on this makeshift lap while his freed hand rifles his pockets for enough coins to pay for the milkshake. Going out the door requires a different tricky negotiation. He will lay her across his saddle, cradled in his arms, and ride away to his derelict hideout in the hills, where she will be his love forever.

Derivative, you'd have to say.

Frances picked up her foolscap pad and her book, put her pen in her handbag. It was getting close to lunchtime. She'd go for another walk first.

She looked at marvellous houses, Federation, deeply verandahed with wooden patterns elaborate as knitting, for sale very cheap in the windows of real estate agents. In Canberra they'd cost a fortune. Were they to exist. Perhaps she should come and live in Goulburn in a Federation house and cook and write there. Of the angst of unemployment and fading farms and love betrayed. Or murdered safe forever.

She tried to buy some mattress ticking, which she planned to use for kitchen curtains. Goulburn would be a repository of the old-fashioned virtues, like mattress ticking. But though she found a dim drapers that almost had a high bentwood chair for its lady customers to sit on, it knew nothing about such a fabric, nor did department stores, or a glossy curtain shop hung with sugar-pastelled art deco drapes.

Back at the cafe, lunchtime rush. Sudden fears of no room. But there was a booth. She ordered a small pizza, Napoletana with garlic and olives and anchovies, and a half-bottle of red wine. With a glass of white straightaway, to drink while she waited.

The waitress is shocked. She's not used to women alone drinking wine. In fact, hardly anybody is doing so. Even the tables of businessmen in white shirts eating the great oval plates of steak and chicken and roast pork are washing them down with cappuccinos.

A friend of mine has a vision of the good life of cafes, of a society that frequents them, meets friends there and makes them, in one black coffee buying hours of conversation. It's a difficult idea to put in practice; the cafes aren't up to it, nor are the friends. Music is allowed, provided it's pure, like jazz. Art on the walls is a good thing. She doesn't care about wine, or cocktails, or even the food, but the coffee should be excellent. And the ambience. The problem is that ambience is difficult to judge, and to agree on. She has trouble keeping her few dogged regulars up to the mark. I meet her sometimes, but can't always be bothered.

This cafe is not at all the sort of place she means. But she'd approve of the writing.

I'm sipping the wine when a young man comes and sits beside me. Well, the cafe is quite full. He's very pale, with a lot of grubby blond curling hair. He's wearing a dinner suit whose silk lapels are frayed and stained. The effect is sickly Dietrich in drag, those throaty songs she used to sing with burning eyes and cigarette smoke in baroque garlands about her. An angel, not so much fallen as slipped.

He sits close on the narrow bench. I feel something pointed in my ribs. I look down. It's a knife. Hey, mind my silk shirt. He lowers it to my hip-bone, where the jeans stretch tight. What do you want?

Money.

I take up my handbag. There's twenty dollars, five, a lot of coins. He looks at it hopelessly.

Why don't I buy you a pizza?

Not hungry.

Are you on drugs?

He turns his sickly slipping face with its burning eyes on me. What makes you think that?

I shrug. Do you write poems?

Why should I?

Michael Dransfield did. He was on heroin and wrote these marvellous poems. *You can't buy much for thirty dollars now*, one's called.

I don't tell him how young he died, or how.

The waitress brings the pizza and the red wine. At least have a little wine, I say, and ask the woman to bring another glass.

I have to go to the toilet, he says, before the glass arrives. He hangs on to the end of the table to pull himself sliding across the seat so he can get out of the booth. These booths are narrow, hard on the bum. You have to scrabble to get out of them. His knife falls to the floor with a tinkle. He sits on the end of the seat and looks at it in despair. I see that he can't imagine crawling under the table to get it. I hook it with my foot towards me, bend down, manage to reach it, and pass it to him, handle first, politely brought up as I was. He's puzzled, for a bit, then puts it in the dinner jacket pocket. Careful, I say, it could stick into you; this too only puzzles him. I realise that his imagination has quite failed him, that the effort to picture himself living his life is too much. Perhaps if somebody else were to take over the picturing . . .

I have to write this down in detail. I hadn't ever understood before that we need to be able to picture our lives in order to live them. That it is only when our brains can imagine performing the most simple of acts, like bending under a table to pick up a knife, that they can give the commands to the nerves and muscles and tendons that will carry out those acts, and shift desire into the past tense. One day even the involuntary behaviour, like breathing, will become too hard for his brain to imagine, and then he'll stop.

The pizza is good, so is the wine. The young man is gone a long time. Should I go out to the lavatories, peer under the door for his feet, see if he's safe? I've kept him some wine.

My imagination isn't strong enough, or maybe not willing, to stand in for his. Even the possible absence of space under the lavatory door defeats me.

Two waitresses bring their lunches to the next booth. They flop down, which squashes the breath out of them in heavy sighs, they rub their backs, kick their shoes off with little hidden clunks. One is reading the *Goulburn Post*.

Any jobs?

The Brown Derby's advertising for a waitress.

How would that be any better than here?

Mm.

The smoke from their cigarettes is drawn uneddying up into the air-conditioning ducts.

The young man is still not back. I pour the rest of the wine in my glass. Perhaps it's physical disease that has enfeebled his imagination. Perhaps he has AIDS. Thin, wan, decadent, in a decayed dinner suit. Life is a cabaret, my friend. Lucky his knife did not pierce me. I am not afraid of his sad breath beside me. I know it needs more than that to infect.

I'd like to have him take the money. I'd like him to be a poet.

A waitress stands a wooden sign several booths nearer the front. I walk around it to read its gilded message: Please Coach People Only. Its multiple syntactical possibilities take my attention. I'm still adding them up when a man brushes past it, to my table. He's handsome in the way I admire; thin, I think, yes, with chiselled nose and cheeks, carved mouth, deep-set eyes, obsidian hair—oh man of stone, oh obdurate man.

Not at all. Not at first. Quite friendly.

May I sit with you?

I flutter my hand in the manner of gracious hostesses. He's wearing a thick large cotton jacket in pearl grey that I immediately covet, with a shell-pink linen shirt; wearing them so easily, these clothes comfortable and forgotten.

He leans forward. Has anybody ever told you how beautiful you are?

Oh, come now, Frances. This is over the top. Nobody ever did or ever will say that to you. Interesting, now, we might believe interesting. But beautiful? In the lurid light of a million fluorescent tubes? Try again.

Do you come here often?

Let's not have the cliché simple either. Well, maybe okay if it's irony. If he's sending up the stereotype. But it's difficult to establish irony in so new a character, even one so admirable of shirt and jacket.

What's a woman—this is good, woman's the right note—woman like you doing in a place like this?

51

Does this mean we're going all out for the irony? Still a bit dangerous. And what place? Goulburn? The cafe? Is the ambiguity useful? And, I mean, we don't want to knock Goulburn. I like it. There's something serious about it. Like Wagga. Places that grew by necessity.

He leans towards me.

The wine looks delicious.

Banal, but not risible. Next?

Another bottle of the red, he says to the waitress.

How about, failed for words, he tries gesture. Reaches forward and picks up my glass, turns it in a half circle, and kisses the oily crescent of my lip's imprint. The while looking at me. Wow.

The waitress brings the wine, and is confused about which glass is whose. He has to give me back the kissed glass, have the clean one put in front of him, approve the label, taste the first drop. Still confused, the waitress doesn't know whether to fill two glasses or one.

Oh no. I'm driving. I shouldn't drink any more. I'll get breathalysed.

Well. Who's being banal now.

Masterful, he takes the bottle, pours me half a glass, raises his in a toast.

To pleasure, he says.

The bright blue eyes gaze out from deep within the chiselled planes of cheek and brow. Perfect lover's face, handsome, attentive, impassioned. But what to do with him? A motel? The car? The banks of—what's the bloody river called? Is there one? Or wandering hand in hand along the street, gazing into the real estate windows. Why not. A Federation house. He can buy one. Set me up in it. A love nest. I cook and write . . . the angst, the anguish, betrayal, whatever . . . He comes, not very often, infrequently enough to keep passion on its toes, to reward longing with bliss, and give plenty of time to get work done in between. Not to mention pop over to Canberra, see Stephen and the kids from time to time.

We have so little time, he says.

And ever at my back I hear . . .

Frances looked at her watch. A quarter to five. The garage closed at five; the car would be shut in after that. She'd have to spend the night in Goulburn. The nights are long in Goulburn. As are the days. The dark night of the soul: what about the lurid day of the soul? The long bright cafe day of the soul?

She'd packed up her pad, put her pen away, was paying, on Visa card, half bottles of wine proving expensive. She stood at the counter while the waitress worked out how to fill in the form. The long day's cafe of the soul. She'd remember it, write it down later. Now she had to run and get the car.

❖ ❖ ❖

part two

Youth

and

Death

and

Age

Cherubs

*S*he can see the bundle reflected in the mirror. It's oblong and lumpy, dirty yellow in colour. The same colour as the shabby gilt frame of the mirror, that large and speckled oval, garlanded with ribbons and roses, cherubs and trumpets. It reflects her own face, too, round and pale like a drowned woman, with crinkled seaweed hair.

The woman in the gilt mirror breaks off a cherub's foot every time she has a birthday. She does it now, pinching the small gilded member between thumb and finger until it snaps off. She has been doing it ever since she began doing it. The *cloisonné* box contains a number of them. It seems likely that she will run out of cherub's feet before she runs out of birthdays, but the unexpected may happen. It might even be welcome. Birthdays sans cherub's foot will lose their savour. Will she want any longer to pick up the *cloisonné* box and rattle in it all the footloose years? All the footling years, footfallen. Footnoted. Footsore years and ten.

There is another possibility: that there are left as many cherub's feet as she will have years. That when they run out so will her birthdays. There's a secret rightness in this that makes her ready to believe it. As though symmetry will be truth. She does not count the number remaining, that would be morbid. Some cherubs have had both fat little feet broken off, disporting completely footless among the roses and ribbons. Some have lost neither, some only one. The fresh white plaster scars age and yellow; with the earlier ones it is necessary to look closely to see whether they are whole or not.

In the mirror her hair has a greenish tint because of the dye in it. She would like somebody to say, what a wonderful colour your hair is, but doubts that she would believe it. She slides a hank of it through her fingers. Maybe, if she tries, she could see it as beautiful. She narrows her eyes, willing beauty to their beholding; a birthday is a day for beauty. Look at this lock, it has the mysterious faint green sheen of the hair of a sea-woman. A woman from Atlantis, Atlantis destroyed by the secrets it knew, look at the narrow-seeing eyes of the woman in the gilt mirror, she knows them too.

But the narrow eyes see the greenish tint of a starling's bosom, portly and worm-hungry, the rusty black of a scarecrow in worn-out mourning clothes. The wise Atlantean woman floats away and drowns in the depths of the guilty mirror. On its surface the yellow bundle quivers and squeaks.

She didn't tell the girl it was her birthday. She wanted to say no, I can't, it's my birthday, but the asking was in such unrefusable terms she'd acquiesced. The girl standing on her doorstep, etiolated as a weed grown under a rock, dressed in fusty black rag-bag garments and metal-studded boots yawning at the sole so you could see her grubby toes like quintupled oysters in a muddy shell. Saying please can I leave him there's no other way. Not in the flat by himself it wouldn't be safe. Please.

The child in the quilted carry-bag, mustard-coloured, shit-coloured in the context, faintly emanant of fashion and coddled trendy middle-class babies a long time ago, among the sprigged flowers worn pale the child has slept till now but now he wakes and squawks.

She takes him out. He's very wet. His yellow jumpsuit is soaked from armpits to toes. She takes it off, and his nappy, leaves him in just a short singlet lying on the bed. There are clean clothes in the carry-bag, and bottles of milk. The child likes the freedom from the nappy, he waves his legs and then is still as though waiting for grace, and pees in a strong arc on the bedcover.

She imagines him gilded, like the cherubs on the mirror, with crisp limbs to break off when the birthdays come, but he's not the right shape. He's limp and thin, sunless like his mother, with none of the juicy baroque flesh that even in plaster the cherubs enjoy. She rubs his legs, holds them for him to kick against, exercising them to make them strong. She had babies once, before they turned into children and then called themselves adults and left home. She knows what to do, provided she doesn't think, provided she disengages her mind and lets her hands do what they know, folding the nappy, pinning it, lifting the small body, supporting the lolling head inside her palm, rocking him against her shoulder when he begins to cry, a thin wailing like the wind in an abandoned house, jiggling on one foot while she sets the bottle in a jug of hot water to warm.

When she's fed him she puts him over her shoulder and

rubs his back till he burps. A small runnel of milk slops out, as though he were a vessel overfilled. She's sitting on a chair in the bedroom with her feet on a footstool so she has a deep lap and is tipped back, comfortable, solid, safe. Gradually she recovers the repletions of baby-tending, the slowness, the idleness, the simply being. The communication of love on which a child grows. She doesn't know his name; it doesn't matter. Endearments are the only address he needs.

She wonders what his mother actually said. Of her babbling words all she understood was the urgency: she had to go, she had to have the baby minded. Standing on the step in her safety-pinned clothes and her gaping boots, pushing her carefully clotted hair out of her eyes. It occurs to the woman that the girl may not come back again, that the stammering hurry may carry her far away from the poky next-door flat, that the bottles and the clean clothes are the baby's dowry.

Gently she rocks, calm and solid like a heartbeat. She looks up and sees her face in the mirror, framed in maimed cherubs marking off the years, her face round and pale like a drowned woman, and fitting in to the curve of her neck the baby held close against the greenish-dyed crinkles of her hair. Happy birthday.

Oysters

'*A* feed of oysters wouldn't be bad,' said Father. He was reading in the paper about new oyster leases at Port Stephens. He always read the first three pages of the paper at breakfast time, with his tea, and finished it after work. The rest of the family were allowed to read it during the day, provided they didn't muck it up.

'Oh, oysters,' said Mother. She didn't like them as much as father did. 'I suppose if we go to the Bay we might manage a few.'

Peta had been surprised by the oysters. They'd seemed a kind of ceremony, counted out carefully on the plates, six for Mother, twelve for Father, lemon squeezed on, pepper shaken, and then the eating, very slowly, one by one. The kids had fish and chips; they were quicker than the oysters. 'You don't chew them,' said Father. 'You just let them slip down your throat.' They watched it happen. 'Will I like oysters when I'm grown up?' asked Sylvia. 'You might. You'll just have to wait and see, won't you.' Peta was glad it wasn't time for her to find out yet. They looked grey. She knew she ought not to think they looked like the snot that hung out of Barry Duncan's nose, but she had, and couldn't stop.

'Are we going to the Bay this year?' asked Tamsin.

'I thought we'd try the lake again. See if we can get Renfrew's cottage. It's got a good boat.'

The lake was early mornings and the light not yet out. The world colourless and dewy, the water the colour of aluminium saucepans, but soft. The boat slid over the surface, the oars made very quiet slow splashes as they pulled it along. The grass was the same metal colour, and the bridge, the holiday houses. The fishing lines had to be baited and dropped over the side, where the ripples tugged at them; while you were doing that the world would brighten, and everything would become its normal day-coloured self. However much you tried, however hard you remembered, you couldn't ever catch the exact moment when it happened.

People who live by the sea like to go to the lake for holidays. The lake is nothing like the sea, though it flows into it only a few miles away. It is very slow and quiet; it seems to be covered with a bowl of silence, and soft noises like the water washing the pebbles or the creak of oars in rowlocks take a long time to arrive. Whereas the sea is all bluster and violence and vigour, the waves of summer crash nearly as loud as the storms. There's always a wind.

The blows of the sea wind are bad enough—see the thin trees hunched against them. But its caresses are insidious. They bring corruption: rot, mould, rust.

'By jove, I'm glad the lab's not here,' says Father. 'It'd be the end of the instruments.'

Every morning he walks to the lab in Hamilton: it takes him forty minutes, and it's far enough away to escape the ravages of the sea air. At home he rubs the suitcase locks with vaseline but still they rust; he paints the weatherboard walls but deep down under the layers the nails weep; their brown tears streak the surface. The chrome of the kitchen chairs festers, the inside brickwork of the front verandah is leprous. Verdigris quickens on brass fittings. Whereas at the lab the metal instruments shine; they lie in oiled cloths or display themselves in glass cases. Father is a dental technician. He makes teeth for people. They can't go straight to him, they must be sent by a dentist with measurements. That's iniquitous; Father is perfectly qualified to do it from scratch, and it would save people a lot of money. But what can you expect with a cove like Menzies running the country; he takes no thought for the ordinary working man. He panders to the rich. Peta thinks of panda bears; it seems an exotic thing to do. Being rich would be oysters whenever you wanted and panda bears and holidays in guest houses. But not desirable; the Bible says not to lay up treasures on earth, because of the moth and the rust corrupting. Though holiday houses seem pretty mothy and rusty too. Maybe that's the dark glass seeing.

Father is a Christian Scientist. He can cure ills by laying on of hands. Peta hasn't needed it much yet, but Tamsin who is at high school and must study hard sometimes gets headaches. She sits at the dining-room table, very quiet, the whole house quiet, her limbs loose, her eyes shut, and Father puts his hands across her forehead, and concentrates. Afterwards Tamsin smiles and says that's much better and goes back to her homework.

Peta thinks often of difference. Not with the Christian Science. She belongs there. Father is the First Reader. He stands behind the wooden pulpit and reads the Lesson–Sermons about

God who is Divine Love and Infinite Good. She belongs by the sea too, but that's more complicated. Living by the sea marks people. When she says, I live at Merewether and people say, At the beach? she knows they know she is different. Even Judy her best friend can make her think this sometimes, though she only lives a few blocks away. Perhaps it's the light, the sticky salt light; you can see it on the landscape, feel it on your skin. Mostly it's a pleasant kind of difference, lucky even. With her name she's not so sure.

'It's a boy's name,' the kids at school call out. 'Boy's name, boy's name.' 'It's not, it's not,' she says, but they don't take any notice. For a long time this enraged her, and she'd shriek with fury: 'Can't you spell! Can't you spell!' And then one day she thought that probably they couldn't, probably they really didn't know that Peta and Peter were completely different names even though they sounded just the same, because when you said them you saw them written in your head, and the separateness was quite obvious. She'd have liked to talk to her parents about it, but didn't, because it might have looked as though she were being critical of the name they'd given her and she didn't want to hurt their feelings. And she wanted to protect them from her problems.

Now she ignores the kids' taunts. Puts on dignity, closes its shell around her, like a glass case, and their little jets of nastiness splash against it, useless as shots from a water-pistol. They run down the outside and she stares at them, quite safe. The danger is herself breaking the fragile shell, from inside; an awkward lunge of the elbow, a slight unco-ordination of the knee, can shatter it and leave her more vulnerable than before in the midst of its shards. Even an odd twist of the mouth can shiver it. She has to take great care, walk and smile with great control when clad in that glassy dignity.

Judy's the one who's best at making her break it. They're digging the deepest hole ever in the sand against the water leaking from the tide, or climbing up the cliff face to see if the shallow hollow just below its brow could really be considered a cave and used as shelter should dangerous circumstances arise, and they're concentrating on this quite difficult task and having jokes and laughing at the same time, and Judy says: 'It really is a boy's name you know. Girls aren't called *Peter*.' And she can't help giving a twitch and her safety is shattered. Judy smiles and knows what she's done; Peta feels her face go funny and can't find the expression to show Judy she doesn't care.

Peta wonders why there aren't such things to be said to Judy. She doesn't know of any, whereas Judy has a whole lot. Old ones, and new ones. Sometimes when she goes to play on Saturday afternoons Judy stands on the front gate and sings: 'I'm not allowed to play with you! I'm going out. You're not.' Once when they squatted down behind the rocks round the headland to do a wee Judy put her face right down and looked up Peta's dress. 'You've got hair on your bottom,' she said.

'I haven't,' said Peta, 'that's not true.'

But Judy still said it.

❖   ❖   ❖

There's to be a toffee day at school so Peta and her mother make stickjaw. Sylvia is only allowed to watch. The sugar boils and bubbles, it goes from pale to brown, the vinegar is dropped in, it seethes up, Mother pours it into the paper cases. Peta sprinkles the hundreds and thousands on. The toffees will sell for a penny to raise money. Cook's privilege: they're allowed one each. Peta sucks it, then pulls it against her teeth, it stretches in and out and winds around, it's maddening the way you can't bite any off, and that's the fun. Finally; stretch, pull, twist, with patience and a knack, a bit comes off and then she can't chew it, it holds her teeth fast together: stickjaw toffee.

'Ow,' she says, with such anguish that her mother comes. A pain is stabbing into her tooth into her gum into her head. She'd never known teeth had feeling before. She'd always thought they were unliving things, like stones.

She will have to go to the dentist, to Mr Grace who is not an exploiting rich dentist because he's a Christian Scientist too. Father sometimes has to explain to people why the healing doesn't work on teeth; once selfishness and malice and hate have done the damage then the teeth need help. The toffees were made for a good cause; it's hard to see how the trouble could have come from them.

Judy tells her what dentists do. They have pliers to pull out your teeth; sometimes they have to kneel on your chest to get a proper grip. They have drills that grind into your jaw; sometimes they slip and go into your brain and bits run out and you're an idiot. 'You already are so it won't matter.' Peta gets mad and pushes Judy so hard she sits down in a slimy-dry rock pool and green moss sticks to her knickers. Afterwards she thinks of anger; perhaps that's where the toothache came from.

◆　◆　◆

Tamsin goes with her to the dentist. They have to catch a bus into town and another to Speers Point; Tamsin's good at buses because of going to school. It will take more than an hour. On the way Peta begins to cry; the tears run out of her eyes and though she turns her head to look out the window Tamsin sees.

'I don't want it to hurt,' she says.

Tamsin looks worried. 'It should be all right. Mr Grace'll have healing hands. That'll take away the pain.'

'Did it hurt when you had your fillings done?'

'Yes, but that was before Mr Grace came. It'll be different with him.'

Tamsin points through the window, there's a good view from the top of the double decker bus. 'Look, that's Speers Point, and round that bay is Renfrew's place; see the bridge?'

'Is that the *lake*? Where we have holidays? Is Mr Grace at the *lake*?'

It doesn't look like holidays. It's every day, people living here. Tamsin is counting the bus-stops after the hotel. A girl from her school makes this trip every day. She doesn't get home till half past five in the afternoon. They get out into the windy sunshine; the spring has gone back to being chilly. It's a suburban street with fences, and a woman sweeping up frangipani flowers.

Mr Grace is a thin man who tries to say jolly things and doesn't know how. His instruments aren't like Father's, solid and safe as tools, they're thin and wicked. The drill zooms inside her head and hurts a lot, exactly as Judy said it would. Afterwards Mrs Grace, who is big and soft and powder-smelling and couldn't have kiddies though she'd have dearly loved to, gives them cordial and coconut slice but Peta shakes her head, her mouth wants to be left alone, so Mrs Grace takes a cup from the dresser, a shallow cup, carved, of a golden colour that shines pink like a pearl shell. 'It's carnival glass,' she says. 'Would you like to have it?'

All the way home in the bus Peta holds the cup in her hands, feeling the carved flowers. She doesn't tell anybody about Mr Grace hurting. Father reads the home study lesson. There is no evil and no pain, only wrong thinking. She wonders what went wrong with her thinking.

To Judy she says, 'It didn't hurt a bit, not a single bingle bit.' She shows her the cup, safely mirrored shut in the china cabinet. 'That cup's not yours,' says Judy at school next day. 'You're a liar.'

◆　◆　◆

Judy and Peta are sitting on Sailor's Rock. The tide's coming in; eventually the Rock will be completely cut off and since this is spring and high tides, submerged. The water is already swirling choppily about it. They have to stay on the Rock till the last moment for getting back. They're wearing shorts and jumpers because it's too cold for swimming; they'll get into trouble if they get their clothes wet.

Judy fiddles with the big rusted iron ring sunk into the rock.

'I was walking along the beach last night. After your bedtime. And there were some men on this rock. They pulled up this ring and a trapdoor opened and they went inside and down some stairs. There was a yellow light shining. Then they shut the trapdoor. They were smugglers. I heard them talking about gold wristwatches.'

'How could they pull this up? There's no crack.'

'Well of course you can't see the crack. It wouldn't be secret.'

Peta knows that this ring belonged to a chain that marked off a little rock-bound beach called the Ladies' Beach, when her mother was a girl. When she says this Judy says, 'Well, how come I saw smugglers going down a trapdoor, huh?' and gives her a shove that nearly knocks her into the water. Truth can't defeat Judy's stories.

Peta lies on her stomach and stares down into the swirling water. There are shells on the pedestal of the rock: oysters. 'My father likes a good feed of oysters. Let's come and get some next weekend.'

'Urk, oysters. Your father must be mad.'

'It's time to go,' says Peta.

'Not yet,' says Judy, and holds her arm tight. When they finally go it's too late, a wave surges round the rock and drenches them to the waist. Judy turns handstands up the beach. 'Ha ha. You're in trouble,' she sings. Peta's mother will be cross. Judy's will smack her. She collapses on the sand, which sticks to her wet shorts. They won't dry now, it's too late in the day. Judy sifts her fingers through the sand, picks up a shell as big as her little thumbnail. 'You know what these are? These are Chinaman's hats. I know a Chinaman in town who'll give you a pound for a thousand of these.'

'Where?'

'Oh, I know. You get them, I'll fix it for you.'

The beach is thickly littered with the shells, thousands and thousands. A pound is a lot of money.

❖   ❖   ❖

At school on Friday Judy says, 'Meet you tomorrow at Sailor's Rock. Don't forget a knife or something.'

'What for?'

'Oysters, idiot. Brain's dripped out through the holes in your teeth.'

Peta wants the oysters to be a surprise so she doesn't ask for a knife. She goes to the bootbox and gets an old one used for scraping mud off shoes. Judy brings a silver object, about eight inches long, with a head on one end and tapering to a point, like a giant pin. It looks like one of Mr Grace's instruments.

'It's an ice pick.'

'What's that?'

'For climbing glaciers. Ice mountains. You stick it in and pull yourself up.'

Peta doesn't think this thin though heavy silver object would be a very good thing to trust your life to on an ice mountain. For oysters it's better than a blunt knife, but neither of them is very good. The oysters at Sailor's Rock are a disappointment; when they look closely there are just the bases, the fish long gone. They go past the baths to the headland, the wildness of the sea is closer here. At one place the water surges under the rock platform and spurts up through a blowhole in a great hail of spray; go near that and you're wet to the skin in an instant.

'See, the oysters are much better here,' says Judy.

There are a lot of them, but they can't get them off the rocks. However hard they lever with pick and knife the oysters stay stuck fast. Judy discovers that she can get the flat top off or bash it in and scrape the fish out of its bottom shell; they haven't got anything to put them in. Peta runs home, creeps on to the back verandah and collects two jam jars. When she comes back Judy's got five oysters sitting on the rock; she gives her two. Peta is sorry to abandon her vision of the oysters shapely on the plate, each in its pearl bed. But they will still taste good.

The sun today is hot. It's hard work. Their fingers are bleeding from pulling at the unwilling shells. By lunchtime there's about an inch of oysters in the bottom of the jars, covered with seawater to keep them fresh. It doesn't look like a feed. Still, there are quite a lot there; thirteen perhaps, or fifteen; Peta shakes the jar a bit to try to count them. The shell fragments and sand move in a different way from the blobs of fish.

Judy holds hers up to the sun. 'Remember the little kid in *National Velvet*? Who kept his spit in a bottle?'

❖　❖　❖

When Peta goes to play on Sunday afternoon Judy says, 'Eaten y'feed of oysters yet?' Peta looks at her. She thinks she ought not to tell her the truth, but she does. 'My mother didn't like the look of them. She said they smelt funny.'

'What'd she do?'

'She took them up the backyard and buried them.'

Judy laughs. 'My mother tipped them down the toilet.'

They stay at Judy's that afternoon and play Monopoly. Her brother who is three years older plays too. It's good fun, except now and then they forget and jab the board with their torn fingers. There's chocolate cake for afternoon tea.

Multitudinous

Teas

Incarnadine

Epilogue

You should of been there, love. You really missed a treat. Phyllis really done her proud. Well, she's always been good to Cheryl. Could of been one of her own daughters, really. And you know Phyllis. Nothing's too much trouble.

She had this pink scheme, see. Everything was pink, with roses. Roses decorating the plates and the table, and a lovely dewy rosebud for all the ladies. She had that tablecloth she embroidered for her own box, remember? Must be thirty years. All over cabbage roses. The work! Took her donkey's years, as I recall. And lacy pink paper serviettes. And of course her Royal Albert were just the thing, and her crazy tea-set, and she borrowed cups and stuff so it'd be all pink and roses. And the pink food! You couldn't of imagined the spread she had, you never seen such food. And all so dainty. Of course, I reckon if food looks nice it's half the battle.

Oh no, the presents wasn't pink. They was wrapped in pink paper, but, Phyllis specially asked. I got her this crinoline lady, china, with a big hoop skirt with blue china bows on, and you lift the side bits off and they're pepper and salt shakers. Real cute. And tasteful.

About twenty, twenty-five, I suppose. The usual crowd. Cousins, aunts, a few girlfriends. Some women from the office. And June of course. She's going to be bridesmaid. Oh no, Ken wasn't there, just at the end, he picked her up. Reckon he'll have to make a coupla trips. He seems a nice boy. Steady.

❖   ❖   ❖

The lounge-room of a pleasant weatherboard cottage in Newcastle, New South Wales, on the twelfth of March 1960. The occasion is a kitchen tea to shower gifts on the forthcoming marriage of Cheryl and Ken.

My hubby always says, don't you ladies just love a good cake fight. Cake fight, he calls it. The cakes always lose, he says. You ladies come out on top every time.

Mind you, with this spread Phyllis's got here, there's not much chance of getting the better of it. I'm stuffed already.

Do have a sandwich. Tomato spread or pink salmon. Yes, it's just ordinary bread—the secret's cochineal. Yes, just mix it with a bit of milk and sprinkle it on and there you are. Yes, they're my roses, that's Cecil Brunner, it's been a mass of bloom all summer.

He wouldn't marry her in front of the high altar you know. Oh no. One of the side chapels. Well, what do you expect? You've got to have standards. And the dress, too. After all, white is for

. . . you know. But he let her have pink, real pale, sort of blush rose. Actually suited her quite well, really, probably better than white. She's always been a pasty little thing. Pity about her having to leave school. Still, she's done all right for herself. Money in his family you know. Oh yes, they're Yumigood Cakes for All Occasions. Very warm. She hasn't done too badly for herself at all.

Don't those cream horns look good. With the pink cream filling. Ooh I must just try one of those. I know it's naughty, but my sweet tooth, I just can't resist.

And your daughter? Got a steady boyfriend yet? Oh she's at university. Ohhhh.

Oh yes, Jan's got a lovely boy. They're announcing their engagement on the sixth of June. It's a secret, but they're lay-bying the ring tomorrow. Oh yes, a diamond. I think a diamond's nice, don't you? More real somehow.

Oh Fay's real well, thanks. Oh yes, she's had the baby. Quite recently. Terribly premmy of course. He had us terribly worried at first, being so early, but he's picked up that fast. Gone ahead in leaps and bounds, all in a matter of days it seems. Oh yes, he's at home now. I'll pop over and see you some time if you like, put him in the pram, give you a look at him. He's a bonza kid. And so bright. You should see his grandfather. Can't get enough of him.

Ooh Phyllis, you're spoiling us. Ooh I really shouldn't. Strawberry and cream sandwiches. Ooh I can't resist.

Yeah, that's right. No, the third. She's already got two. Well, not surprising, you not being upterdate, I mean. She's pretty fast off the mark. You know, if this one turns up only a week early she'll have three under the age of two? Not bad, eh?

Oh yes, catherlicks, couldn't you guess. All I can say is, try giving the Pope three little kiddies in nappies to deal with and he'd pretty soon change his views on you-know-what.

Still, on the other hand, they could go a bit easier, couldn't they, if you know what I mean. I mean, three in two years, what are you going to make of that? Still, I'm glad none of mine married a mick.

I said to her, I said you'd be real silly to get married now, when you're twenty. Wait another six months, until you've had your birthday. I mean, you can't have a proper twenty-first when you're a married woman. It's not the same thing, somehow. People don't take it so seriously.

Oh yes, the engagement party was lovely. About sixty all told. In the church hall, Marj and I did the supper. Quite a nice spread really. She got some lovely things. People were real good to her. You should see her box. She's a lucky girl.

Oh yes, I'd love some more tea. Nothing like a good cuppa. These get-togethers with the girls always give you such a thirst.

Pink lamingtons. However do you do it. I must get the recipe. And coconut ice. Ooh I can't choose. I must just have one of each. Ooh greedy me.

And the butterfly cakes. The work. Those pink sugar wings, with the silver cachous. So dainty.

We're not sure where we'll be at first, have to get a flat somewhere, I suppose. But we've just put a deposit on a block of land. Out at Redhead. A bit far out, but Ken says that area's really going to go ahead. And it's quite a big block. Oh yes, Ken's keen to have a garden. Grow all our own vegies. And down the back he's going to plant some of those pine trees,

what are they called, um, *penis radiata*. He says they'll be a real
investment in thirty years' time.

Did I ever tell you what happened to poor Myra? Well, it
was just before her wedding, and she'd been to the doctor to
see about . . . birth control, and all that . . . you know, and
afterwards she went to this pantry tea, organised by a cousin
or someone, and there was this really ancient aunt, well, great
aunt really, up from Sydney, sort of guest of honour. The original
maiden aunt, you know the kind of thing. Lavender and old
lace in person. Anyway, Myra was handing round the tea, and
this aunt's a bit deaf, so Myra goes up to her and shouts at
the top of her voice—lean a bit closer, I don't want anybody
to hear—poor Myra goes up to her and shouts, "Do you want
your contraceptive now, Aunt Sylvia?" Talk about die!

Do have some jelly—I'll let you into a secret, I've put a drop
of port into it, so we'll all be tipsy. Oh Aeroplane. Yes, I always
buy Aeroplane. They might cost a bit more but they're worth
it, I reckon. Always sets, and such a good colour.

Have some ice-cream. Vanilla, actually, but I just put a
drop of cochineal in, and stirred in some of those crystallised
cherries.

She looked *awful*. The neck of her dress was so low you
could practically see her navel. And she was wearing one of
those jelly-on-a-plate bras—I know, isn't it awful, but Myra says
that's what they call them—you know the kind that push you
right up from underneath and you wobble. Well, you should
of seen the boys flocking round her, you know how they always
go for that sort of thing. Cheap. Well, if that's what you've got
to do to catch a man. Mind you, you won't catch anything

much that way, either, after all no decent man's going to want his future wife making a show of herself like that, is he.

Oh no, not engaged yet. 'D suit me if they never was. She leads him a right old dance. Mind you, I could of told him that, first time I set eyes on her. You're a hard one, my girl, I said to meself. Good looking, of course. Them's the worst.

Yes, that's the people. Live in Bar Beach, that big blue and white house. Nothing but the best. He owns that Men's Outfitters bottom end of town. Plenty money, o' course, but that's not everything, just makes for waste I say. You know she likes to be taken out for tea in restaurants Sat'dy nights? What about Sundy night tea at home I says to Brian. Good enough for ya brother and sister. Oh no, Mum, he says, Amanda likes to dine out in restaurants, it's much more fun. How can a boy ever put by a deposit when he's forever taking some girl gadding in restaurants, I ask you. And unhealthy—you never know where the food's been. Give me good honest-to-goodness home cooking any day.

Don't mind if I do, thanks. Pink and white neenish tarts. Isn't that clever. I never seen such a spread as you got here, Phyllis.

I'm dying to see what Cheryl's got in her box. You can tell a lot about a girl from her glory box. June's got some truly lovely things, but then she started collecting when she was hardly more than a kid. Fifteen and her first pay packet, as I recall. Six pairs of sheets she's got already, she's always put things on lay-by, towels and tablecloths, and pillowslips she's been embroidering, with His 'n' Hers and lovebirds and things, she's real good with her needle, and a set of saucepans and a dinnerset and some really lovely cutlery with flowers down the handles, oh, a stack of stuff. I like to have a couple of lay-bys going, Mum, she says. You don't really miss the money and the things mount up. And that's another thing. I was never so pleased when things didn't work out between she and Reg; the best thing that could have happened you giving him the chop, my girl, I told her. He's a bit of a drifter, Reg, a boy like that could never give a girl a steady home. I was never really happy with the engagement you know, but June was that keen I hadn't the heart.

Whoever told you that? Good heavens no. June decided he wasn't right for her. Oh yes, I know he's taken up with the Roberts girl, but you know how these things happen on the rebound. She's welcome to him, as far as I'm concerned. Some girls are no better than they ought to be, if you ask me.

You know that Fay? June was her bridesmaid last year, she had a lovely ballerina, layers and layers of aqua tulle, well you should of seen her box showing. Brought out the trewso as well. Well, you should of seen it—black lace panties, scanties rather, hardly there, you could of seen *everything* through them. And a black nylon nightie with red ribbons, *completely* transparent. Would of left *nothing* to the imagination. Not at all a suitable thing for a bride. Well, I mean to say, it made you wonder, a girl like that. And now, well, it just goes to show, doesn't it, turns out *they* didn't wait for the wedding night. Be sure your sins will find you out, I always say.

Just look at that cake. Heart-shaped. Isn't that just the right thing? Oh yes, Phyllis made that too. She's been going to Tech you know, doing cake decorating, started after the girls left home, done all the advanced courses. She made Fay's wedding cake too, all four tiers, and I s'pose she'll do Cheryl's as well. Doesn't she do a beautiful job? Look at the roses, you'd swear they

were real. And the lattice work. And look at the pink lace—
the patience. It's a shame to cut it. Should keep it and just
look at it.

I do like the pink theme, don't you? I remember Fay had
a marigold one, everything sort of yellow. Very pretty, but the
pink's nicer. I know I shouldn't but I can't help thinking of
stinky bills when I think of marigolds. Course Fay just had
the one. This is the sixth I've been to for Cheryl: pantry, bathroom,
cellar, two kitchens, and what was the other one? There must
be another one. I'm sure there've been six. Pantry, bathroom,
cellar, two, or maybe it's three kitchens, perhaps that's it.

Don't mind if I do. I'm partial to a bit of fruit cake. Especially
when it's a nice dark moist one. And almond icing. I love almond
icing.

Dad gave me the camphor wood chest to keep m' things
in. Doesn't it smell lovely? You can put blankets in it afterwards,
and it makes a really nice piece of furniture. Of course not
all m' box fits in it, and I don't put the china and all in, and
not m' collection of cut crystal. I've got nine pieces now, they're
on the sideboard in the dinette. We can all go and look at
them after supper. Mum says she'll be glad when I've gone and
take all m' stuff with me and she's got room to breathe in her
own house.

Oh, aren't these gorgeous. Oh, I love crinoline ladies. They're
absolutely adorable, really the nicest pepper and salt shakers
I've ever seen. And the teatowels, what beaut linen, and the
little dogs are so cute, how did you know they were just what
I want? And the honey spoon, look how it twirls, I haven't
got a honey spoon. Oh, and look, an eggtimer, no excuse now
for not getting Ken's eggs just right. And the beautiful potholders,
blue and yellow's the colours I'm having for the kitchen, gosh

you're good at crosher. What pretty spice jars: thyme, and basil, and oregano, gee I have to learn to cook. What can this be . . . the *Commonsense Cookery Book*, fabulous, sounds just like me. And a ladle, and wooden spoons, and measuring cups. Terrific. Kitchen scales, aren't they fabulous. And a scone tray, and cake tins and an eggbeater. You all know just what I need. Terrific, a potato peeler and a sharp knife—ooh, is it ever. Golly, I just have to learn to cook and invite you all over to supper one night. Won't be near as good as this but. This is just fabulous. And you've all been so good to me. I'm so lucky, getting such fabulous presents. I can't wait to start using them all.

Oh Auntie Phyllis I think a rose tea's just lovely.

Roses roses all the way. Rosy dreams of nuptial bliss. Rosy food for rosy futures. Feasts for eyes of rosy morsels. Rosy brides turn rosy mums of rosy babies.

Oh Phyllis it's so pretty. Isn't it sweet. I love the pink. Oh Phyllis how do you *do* it? Pink sandwiches. Pink cakes. Pink tarts. Pink buns. Pink scones. Pink biscuits. Oh Phyllis you are a wonder.

And a quivering pink jelly blushing on a plate. Take, eat . . . sacramental flesh for the grinning marriage rites. Eat, eat, aunts and cousins married women high priestesses of the cult. And the novices boxes ready eagerly awaiting. Waiting to be initiated. Waiting to be worshipped. To be sacrificed. Waiting to be showered with presents and eaten up. Pink tongues sipping at pink flesh. Pink tongues pink food quivering flesh of blushing virgins ha ha ha that's a laugh give her the benefit of the doubt the proof of the pudding is the bun in the oven.

Oh Phyllis a rose tea. Oh how pretty oh how sweet I must do one tell us Phyllis tell us . . .

I must do one for Jan. And for June. And for Anne, and Betty, and Carol, and Diane. For Wendy and Xanthe and Yvonne and Zoe. It's such a success.

Multitudinous teas incarnadine.

Tell us Phyllis tell us.

Cochineal and carmine and crystallised fake cherries. A million coccus cacti dried and crushed. Artificial colouring artificial flavouring essence of raspberry essence of strawberry essence of roses. Synthetics. Additives. Certified food colouring. Chemical numbers in a catalogue.

Arsenic and red lead? Oh no never, never no more. That was the nineteenth century. We know better now. Nothing poisonous, not any more. Guaranteed harmless. Guaranteed healthy.

Pretty. Pretty.

Death
and the
Mother

*W*hen Maria Laker in Paris received a letter from a friend at home, she was sitting at the breakfast table with a novel. It was *Crime and Punishment*; she was re-reading the Russians. Last time she'd been in her teens; she wanted to see if the decades had changed them, or her. She hoped the latter. So far she was immersed, couldn't put it down. Except for a letter from home.

It was a long one: ten pages. After three of them she dropped it on the table and went into the kitchen. No more coffee. She came back to the dining-room. She looked at the cream onion-skinned notepaper, imagined Celine's red-nailed fingers scrawling her shapeless words. She hunched her shoulders and pulled her dressing-gown round her; the central heating was turned high but even leaning against the radiator didn't warm her up. Her chest was concave with cold.

'Do you remember,' Celine wrote, 'a boy called Hugh Temple?' Maria didn't, but that didn't matter. 'About the same age as Jonathan, or maybe fifteen, I think he might know him, I think they might have gone to primary school, they live just behind the school. Anyway poor child was riding his bike and skidded on the wet road and went under a truck and the wheels went over him the truck's and he's had to have both legs amputated poor kid and still endless operations.'

Maria felt it, she was the mother feeling the child's pain, the mother feeling the child's legs crushed and not able to save him. She leant against the radiator and looked at the room, pretty hired room, not seeing the imitation Louis XV furniture or the yellow velvet curtains or the painted wooden panelling. She stood and stared and felt her eyes become enormous and glassy, like television screens showing bad news, the sort of news that makes people say it shouldn't be allowed, it is an insult to the dignity of human beings to pry into the intimate details of their misery. She shook her head to shift the focus; there was the letter on the table, Jonathan's plate smeared with butter and raspberry jam and beside it the crumb of the bread that he always discarded so he could eat more of the crust, Geoff's half full milk-congealed teacup, the Penguin *Crime and Punishment*, literature so much easier to bear than life, which she'd put down when she heard the postman's clatter. She saw the untidiness and began to order it.

The tulips on the mantelpiece were really too far gone. The elegant pointed flowers had snapped open, flinging petals across the carpet, or hanging limply from the stems exposing not very pretty private parts. The water smelt bad, they were decaying. She collected all their litter into a plastic bag and threw it away. She hated throwing away flowers. Geoff would say, aren't those tulips somewhat dead? and she would reply, not quite, look, this one is rather pretty still, and that; they'll last a bit longer. It seemed cruel to enjoy flowers while they were fresh, in their brightest bloom, and then reject them at the first sign of age. As if they were, like people, deserving of affection though no longer young, all the more so because of the pleasure they'd once given. But these tulips had to go.

She made more coffee and tried Celine's letter again. 'And do you remember the Hensons, you met them at our place just before you went away, he's in Trade, their son was killed, just last week, riding his motorbike, he was in first year at uni, not his fault the guy in the car was in the wrong but that's not much consolation . . .'

She remembered the Hensons, the dinner at Celine's. Carl hadn't been there, but how his parents had evoked him. Their only beloved brilliant child. And now he was killed instantly. So Celine wrote. She considered the word instantly, whether people said it to comfort; it seemed as formulaic and terrifying as a *memento mori*. The parents' grief would be instant too, but not finite. Maria thought it would be better to die as well; without your child you wouldn't really be alive, you'd be a zombie, dead but not allowed to leave the earth. She imagined herself without Jonathan, crawling through her life like a maggot in a wound.

Why was Celine offering this macabre gossip? The flimsy expensive sheets of paper had carried this burden of misery twenty thousand kilometres. Like the song: Pass it on, pass it on. Except that was happiness, the knowledge of salvation. Maria looked at the purple ink, the shapeless words hard to decipher. Was there a kind of celebration in their lumpy flourishes? Celine smug about her own children surviving, a finite store of pain being handed out to others, being used up, none left for her.

Maria had no faith in the finiteness of grief. If it could happen to others, it could happen to her. You could not scribble it down on paper and send it away. Carl Henson, Hugh Temple, could not save Jonathan Laker.

She went back to the letter, thinking masochism, but there were no more horrors. Celine prattled on about the drought and the hideous long summer, about carpeting the house and the wines they'd just bought: 'We're not supposed to drink them till the year two thousand, hope we live long enough to enjoy them, you and Geoff better make sure you're around to help us.'

When Jonathan came in for lunch she had been to the market and bought another dozen tulips and some black pudding, which was cooking with onions and apples. It was easy to please Jonathan with food. His dark blond hair was ruffled all over his head. She kissed his smooth flushed face, now on a level with her own, thinking soon I shall have to stand on tiptoe to reach.

— What icy cheeks, she said. You've given me frostbite. I wouldn't have thought it was that cold out.

— It's not. I came home on Sebastien's moped. He gave me a lift. Gosh, Mum . . .

Maria's eyes went large and glassy as television screens.

— You what . . . my God . . . you didn't . . . not in this weather . . . the ice, the slush, the slippery roads . . .

— But Mum. Mum. Mopeds are perfectly safe. Perfectly safe. They only go about ten kilometres an hour. And Sebastien's got a spare crash helmet he's going to lend me.

— Oh no he's not. No. No. Because you're not going on it again. Do you hear? Do you understand? No more riding on mopeds. I won't have it.

— But Mum. Why? They aren't dangerous. All the kids have them. You don't even need a licence. They're only fifty ccs you know, or less. And terrifically solid.

— But people aren't, said Maria. Anyway, I'm not arguing. I've said what's to be and that's that. She closed her eyes, to signify by blindness that she was deaf as well, and every time Jonathan tried to say something she shook her head and squeezed her eyes more tightly shut and repeated, There's no more to be said.

After lunch she gave him Celine's letter to read. He vaguely remembered Hugh Temple, or thought he did; perhaps he had gone to St Brigid's, not the local primary school. He was shocked by what had happened to him, but briefly; he was fourteen, he didn't identify with the fates of others.

— You see why I say no mopeds?

— But that's got nothing to do with it. That wouldn't happen to me. Mopeds are very safe, they've got wide tyres, they don't skid. And Sebastien is very careful, and so would I be.

— So I daresay was this poor child. And the Henson boy— Celine says it wasn't his fault. The point about an accident is that it's just that, accidental. Nobody *means* to have an accident, it's something that *happens* to them, they can't *help* it.

She could see that Jonathan did not believe this. He thought that he could control what happened to him. That whatever became of others he would be the skilful master of his destiny. Once again Maria had to close her eyes and shake her head and say I am not prepared to argue.

That night she had her double-decker bus dream. She wasn't quite asleep when it happened, but she had no control over it. It unrolled in her head, like a film she was forced to watch, she had no power to stop it. She knew it was a dream, and that made it worse, as though her own mind were deliberately torturing her.

It came from a time they were living in Cambridge and Jonathan who was nine then had to go quite a long way to school. Part of it was through a park called Christ's Pieces which was pleasant, but after that he had to cross Jesus Lane, a very busy street and curved so that speeding cars and trucks were upon you before you saw them; its name seemed an expletive, a blasphemy rather than a blessing. But worst of all was the first bit, down Parker Street, which was very narrow and with footpaths about half a metre wide, and the great red double-decker buses thundered along it to and from their terminus in Drummer Street, just by the entrance to Christ's Pieces. The buses thundered past, and pedestrians pressed themselves close against the high grey walls of Emmanuel College but still felt the hot wind of their passage, the roar and suck of the air that tried to snatch them under the wheels. Sometimes if the buses passed one another in particularly narrow places these huge black wheels mounted the footpath and then the pedestrians crushed themselves flat against the walls and wondered what had saved them. Jonathan was quite old enough to make his way to school but it was too hazardous. Every morning and evening Maria went with him. She pressed him against the wall of Emmanuel, against the barred windows of the basement laundries which gave off the sweet industrial smell of soap powders, putting her body between his and the black wheels that were taller than he was, seeing the complicated pattern of their deeply indented treads as they trundled past her. The great black wheels got into her mind and she couldn't get rid of them. Whenever afterwards he was late or she'd been quite mildly worried about where he was a big red bus would lumber through her mind and crush him, and the tall black wheels would roll past her and she'd have to look into the deep patterns of the treads and see what was there . . . In the daytime she could say to herself, You are neurotic, you are paranoid, and turn the gaudy image of destruction back into a quite useful means of transport, but not at night, not in the throes of that inexorable conscious dreaming.

She never dreamt of busy green Paris buses though now she dwelt among them. They hadn't lived in Cambridge for years and

Jonathan had come no closer to being run over by a double-decker bus than her fear of it, but she couldn't dismiss it. Double-decker bus. A funny name for a nemesis, a child's name, a jolly name, alliterative and jingly, and the object bright coloured, a friendly feature of English life. Jonathan had had a toy red double-decker bus when he was three; he'd loved it and been heartbroken when he lost it. They'd searched all about the place for it, and never found it, and not till much later did he tell her that he'd posted it down the garbage chute from their tenth floor flat. He'd been curious to hear the noise dropping down, and hadn't realised for quite a long time, not till after all the vain searching in fact, that he would not be able to get it back. For years he shook his head sadly over that childish folly.

Red double-decker buses make comic songs. Flanders and Swann sing one, about a London omnibus. Very humorous, they make it. Its size, and the number of its wheels—six—its scarlet paint, its diesel engine and quantity of horsepower. Ninety-seven. Maria imagined ninety-seven horses. Enormous horses with iron hooves and all their galloping power turned into one great dreadnought. The monarch of the road, Flanders and Swann call it, silent monarch, ninety-seven soundless inescapable horses. It's a song for singing in a deep voice, rumbling and lumbering, and the bus that lurched through her dreams sang it too, but falsetto, which made it very sinister.

❖   ❖   ❖

Jonathan didn't have gut feelings about red buses, he'd quite enjoyed the close-up view of the black wheels and the oily things underneath, just this now faint regret for the handsome toy he'd lost. He was much more concerned with the undermining of his present projects. Coming home on the back of Sebastien's moped had been meant to be the thin end of a wedge, not the collapse of all his hopes. His mother was to have been infected with his own excitement, she was good at that, she entered into his enthusiasms quite happily; mildly of course in typical adult fashion, but thoroughly, taking pleasure in his pleasure. She was to have understood the joy of even the feeble speed of a moped, the wind in your face, the control of your own motion. Then he would have begun on mopeds generally and what excellent things they were, and next mentioned the fact that there was one for sale on the bakery window, only 380 francs, hardly more than fifty dollars, an amazing bargain, he could be independent, need no longer take the train to school, it would certainly save money in the long run, in fact quite soon, and they would not even have to buy a helmet since Sebastien had a spare, and it would cost almost nothing to run, mopeds run on practically spoonfuls of *essence*. She would of course demur, and disapprove, and question, but in the end, faced with this sort of dazzling argument, she would reluctantly but gracefully agree, especially with a bit of encouragement from his father whom he'd work on separately, and there he would be, master of his own fate, or at least his movements.

At dinner he said:

— You know, trains are rather dangerous things.

— Sure are, if you get in their way, said his father, grinning as if he'd made a joke.

— You can't always help it, said Jonathan darkly.

Maria's attention was like a swift sharp blade from the hand of a circus knifethrower. What do you mean? Jonathan, you haven't . . .

— No Mum, I haven't. I just mean that trains aren't necessarily the safest form of transport, they can have accidents, can't they?

— Pretty rarely, said Geoff. Hardly ever, really. After all, they run on tracks, to timetables, and are driven by professionals, and all that. Not like cars, belting all over the place, in the hands of the most God-awful amateurs. In this country. I should think, statistically, you're probably safer travelling by train for a year than by car for a day.

Maria knew this argument too, and believed it, academically, and more viscerally when Jonathan was out in other people's cars, and no doubt would with absolute passion when he came to drive a car himself. But she didn't actually worry much when they were all three out driving together. She was equally calm on aeroplanes, on those thirty-hour treks from one side of the world to the other; she no longer feared even the illogical steep ascent from the ground. Perhaps it was a case of *We'll all go together when we go*. It was not death she feared so much as grief.

—You reckon? said Jonathan.

—Well, it's a guess. But I bet there's some sort of huge discrepancy like that.

—Jonathan, said Maria, have you been crossing the line again?

Jonathan's brain searched for some non-lying, non-incriminating answer, and failed.

—Oh, I mostly get there in plenty of time, these days.

—And when you don't, you go under the gates.

—It's perfectly safe. I only do it when the trains aren't coming. The gates go down such ages before. I know what I'm doing.

Maria was aware of the earliness of the gates too, and had her own criterion: if you heard the bell that signified the closing of the level crossing it was safe to duck under the barriers to reach the platform on the other side; that way you wouldn't miss the train, the metro into Paris. Nothing more maddening than waiting legally for minutes at the crossing with no train in sight knowing that you would miss it when it finally did come. There was a bridge over the lines, but further up the track; you didn't have time to go that way. So anyone not decrepit nipped under the gates and across the lines. Looking to the right, though that direction was safe enough, since you could see the train stopped only a few yards away and trust the driver not to run you over, and then more carefully to the left where the line curved out of sight a hundred metres away or more. Everybody did it. Maria included. There was a notice that said:

ADULTS

DO NOT CROSS THE BARRIERS

CHILDREN ARE WATCHING YOU

but nobody was admonished by it. Presumably everyone did as Maria did; crossed the lines and forbade their children to do so.

— I wonder are all children so determined to wipe themselves out, said Maria.

— Gosh Mum, this *aligot* is great tonight. *Chouette. Formidable.* He scooped up the potato, twirling it round his fork to break the long tendrils of melted cheese, rolling it over his tongue and pressing it against his palate, a parody of a gourmet. Maria smiled, perceiving the diversion, but still pleased.

— I see that red herring tastes quite good too, she said, and they all laughed. The diversion had worked, Maria for the time being stopped fussing about trains.

◆　◆　◆

The next day, coming back from the market with a basket full of vegetables and cheeses and little treats of *pâté* for lunch and a real rooster to make *coq au vin*, she had to wait at the level crossing. She wasn't in a hurry and didn't consider ducking under the barriers. She put the basket down and leant her elbow on the post supporting the gate. She stared at the shabby chateau across the way, really seeing it, as she liked to do in foreign places, its peeling blue paint and blotched cream walls. It was a *gentilhommière*, a gentleman's residence, pompous name, especially now it was a home for unmarried mothers. It had had its moments of glory; Péguy had started his pilgrimages to Chartres from there. Apparently that was a moment of glory. In 1912. Her eyes moved to the chestnut trees behind, green and bosomy, and already showing the faint creamy wax of the coming blossom. Paris and the candles of the chestnut flowers in spring. Candles: everyone called them that, it was corny, but she could never think of a more original description. She was trying when the train came through. The concussion of its speed seemed to knock her backwards. She'd forgotten about the train, though she was waiting for its passage, and it made her heart jump with fright, yet it was going fairly slowly, braking to stop at the station beside the crossing. She watched the dozens of metal wheels gobbling up the rails. Imagined crossing the line at the last minute and getting a foot stuck in one of the grooves . . . Jonathan running late across the line his shoe slipping into the groove sticking the shoe caught the foot with it snatching at the laces scrabbling pulling trapped the driver slamming on his brakes the shriek the foul smell of burning asbestos no chance not a hope . . . .

That night a big red double-decker bus out of a comic song lumbered through her dreams and crushed her son with its black elaborately treaded wheels. She woke with sick terror flowing in her blood and through the networks of nerves and muscles, and even the spaces between her fingers ached.

❖   ❖   ❖

The Lakers thought of themselves as living in Paris and they did in a way but in the suburbs, about twenty kilometres from the actual small city, in a green and wooded valley attached to the capital by a thread of train line, which called itself the metro though it ran on the left, and turned the valley into a commuter land. There were a few blocks of flats, some hideous high-rise towers, and a lot of *pavillons*, houses in gardens, very suburban and in places village-like. The Lakers' house had half an acre of lawn and lilacs and roses and a giant pink tamarisk, as well as gnarled and richly fruiting cherry trees, blackcurrant canes, rosemary bushes and espaliered apricots and pears. The best of both worlds: the amazing city half an hour down the line and this opulent garden to hand. Only five minutes to the station and a train every fifteen minutes, mostly.

The trains ran parallel to their street and a row of houses away. You could see the carriages flashing past from the dining-room window. They were noisy, but that didn't matter; you heard their racket and knew Paris was there when you wanted it. Maria reading her breakfast novel was able to mark the passing of time by them. Sometimes there was a melancholy sound of horns to be heard, not hooters or sirens, not electrical or electronic noises, but the musical blast of a real horn, the kind of horn that you wind . . . is wound. Like the horn of Roland, sounded too late in warning of the treachery of the Saracens. *Dieu! que le son du cor est triste au fond des bois* . . . God! How sad is the sound of the horn in the depths of the woods . . . Out on the railway line somebody would wind a horn, there would be a more distant repeating note, and a train would go speeding through. It was the workmen who were repairing the line warning one another of the train's approach. At the end of the day you could see them going home, in their blue cotton working clothes, carrying the large looped brass instruments hung over their shoulders and under their arms, like medieval huntsmen. Maria loved the sound of the horns, the musical melancholy ancient note calling down the wooded valley. They made her think of the musicians of the Apocalypse, the small old men blowing their horns to herald the Last Judgement, carved in stone in the twelfth century around the tympanum of the church of Saint Lazare in Avallon. Lazarus: one of the few who have already experienced apocalypse, since his grave opened and he came forth, but on his own, not with the rest of dead humanity. Maria wondered what he said, and whether anybody had written it down. People must have asked him what it was like to die, what it was like being dead. Did he say? Was he able to? Maybe he was suffering so much from shock that he was unable to remember let alone talk about what he'd known. It was irritating of the Bible not to discuss these things. She'd noticed that a lot of French churches were named after Lazarus; people must have expected something from his patronage. Or perhaps it was just the comfort of that return from the grave.

There was a railway station named after him, too, Gare Saint Lazare, but it was difficult to see that as anything but accidental.

The warning horns on the line seemed to work. Their sounds came quite often. Whenever she heard them she thought of the little old men whose stone breath has for eight centuries blown the last trump to all who regard the church of Saint Lazarus in Avallon.

◆　　　◆　　　◆

Jonathan brought up mopeds again at dinner. I'm afraid that one on the bakery window will go, he said. It's too good a bargain to last long. Maria shrugged. Jonathan waited till the soup was eaten, and said:

— See a man was killed in the metro the other night.

His parents looked at him.

—Got pushed under a train. Rush hour. By a *clochard*, I think. He wasn't sure whether bringing in tramps was a useful detail or not. Well, you know how crowded the platforms are in rush hour, and how people surge forward.

—Oh God, how awful. Maria's imagination was working on the scene.

Jonathan helped it along. Just an ordinary person, going home from work. Got pushed off the platform just as the train was coming in. The people around got, um, er, splashed, he said in a small voice. He didn't actually know this, he'd read it in a thriller, but when he and Sebastien had talked about it they'd agreed it would have been like that.

—Jonathan, that's enough. It's bad enough that it should happen without you being . . . *ghoulish* about it. Geoff was angry. Maria shook her head, a brief tight appalled gesture, as though she could shake the idea of this sudden undeserved death from her mind.

—Sorry, said Jonathan. He tried to cheer his parents up by telling them about the terrifically hard grammar test for which he'd got seventeen out of twenty, the highest mark in the class. Maria thought of death and cleverness, of course a clever child was not more susceptible, not more marked by fate, not more likely to be a victim of malignant chance than a dull one. She wondered if it would have been safer to have had an ugly and stupid child.

❖ ❖ ❖

Maria was going to town to see the Manet exhibition. At lunchtime she complained that by the time she got into town and actually into the Grand Palais, she'd heard the queues were horrific, and barely glanced at the paintings, it would be so late that she'd end up coming home in the very worst of the rush hour and wouldn't get a seat on the train and what a bind that would be. She was really talking to herself about this, as though putting the irritation into words would get rid of it. And it was her own fault; she should have gone in the morning but had sat too long over *The Brothers Karamazov* at breakfast.

—Well, you know how to get a seat, don't you, Jonathan said. You go to Châtelet, and stand close to the edge of the platform and when a train comes in—this only works if it's not our train that comes first—you watch where the doors are and you stand there and then when our train comes in the doors will be in the same place and you can get on first and get a seat.

—Do you do that?

—Oh yes. It always works.

—Marvellous, said Maria. Terrific. Superb. So you stand on the edge of the platform and when the crowd surges forward or some drunken *clochard* lurches against you, fantastic, there you are, pushed under the train, and, and, *splashing* people.

—Well, I don't stand that close. I'm very careful. I know what I'm doing, Mum.

—Know what you're doing? That's a joke, that is, the best joke I've ever heard. I don't think you have the faintest notion what you're doing. You're not fit to be out, you should be on a harness, I shouldn't let you out of my sight . . . Her voice trailed away. She could talk, she could tell, she could warn, harangue, threaten, extract promises, but she couldn't save him. Couldn't stop him. Couldn't stop herself knowing the child's bright beauty was an irresistible enticement of all the worst that fate could do.

—You worry too much, Mum. I'm very careful, you know, you trained me to be, I can look after myself. I don't want to come to a bad end, do I? That's why I could be trusted on a moped, you wouldn't catch me doing anything silly.

She put her arms round him and held him very tight, as though storing up the feel of his self-sufficient body so long removed from hers and the time when she could protect him from harms. You're an idiot, she said, tenderly, an absolute idiot, and he hugged her in return, enjoying the sense of power that having a mother almost smaller than he was gave him, squeezing her as though he could protect her from all alarms. I know, he said, but you're quite fond of me, just the same.

❖ ❖ ❖

There were no apocalyptic horn blasts on the line that day. It was temporarily anyway in good repair. Maria travelled into town uneventfully. The Manet exhibition was brilliant, though terribly crowded, and every time you stood back a bit to take in a painting somebody stood in front of you and you had to manouevre to see it. It was very tiring. She walked from the Grand Palais to the Quai, and after a long wait in a chilly bus shelter by the silver-grey heaving river got a bus that took her past the Louvre to Châtelet, where she went underground and after negotiating a series of passages and escalators and moving footpaths finally achieved the platform her train would leave from; a complicated exercise but worth it if she got a seat and didn't have to stand up all the way home.

She had Jonathan's advice in mind, her own version. She'd watch for the place where the doors opened, but not from very near the edge. The platform was crowded with people. The next train terminated before her station, there would be a wait. Her feet ached with so much walking, and still standing; the seats were all full. She saw the push the falling just as the train came thundering in, quite fast because electric trains can decelerate quickly, braking, slowing, but only in time to come to a stop at the end of the platform, too fast to stop when the driver saw the falling figure. She could think, if it's me it's not Jonathan. Me not Jonathan, and all her fears over. Safe at last from grief.

A woman who'd seen would say, *She looked so surprised.* Poor bystander who sweated and shivered with shock and closed her eyes to the stains that splashed her camel-coloured coat. *She looked so surprised*, she said. *But she smiled. Yes she smiled. She looked so pleased. Yes pleased. Why would she look so pleased,* the woman would say as she drank the tea of kindly strangers and shivered and sweated with shock.

Maria knew. Her imagination played this death over and over again, like a piece chopped out of a movie and thrown on the cutting-room floor, a long unwanted thread of film retrieved by a curious amateur who obsessed plays it over and over again. The one scene, over and over again. Her own death under the asbestos-stinking wheels of a grimy blue train which would have taken her home to a house in the suburbs where a small family waits dinner till she comes.

Decay

*T*he smell in the fridge was becoming impossible to ignore. The knob of charcoal that she'd saved from the fire didn't seem to be doing its job of absorbing it. Perhaps she ought to clear it out. George used to complain of her habit of saving left-overs. Use them or throw them away, he would say, over and over. No, she replied, finally, I like to put them in the fridge for a fortnight and then throw them away. It probably wasn't a fortnight now; maybe a month.

At the back, behind almost empty jars of honey and drying jam and quite recent pickled cucumbers was a plastic-wrapped packet; something creamy covering the inside made it opaque. When she unwrapped it it turned out to be a lamb chop, soft, pink, putrescent, with a green bloom to it. She poked it with her finger, I expect it would be very tender, she thought. Well hung. Game is supposed to be eaten like that. Her daughter had told her about eating crumbling green grouse, at the table of a Lady. Did she like it? Not really, but that was how it was supposed to be. This chop smelt rotten, rich; was it a bad smell, she wondered. People always shuddered, wrinkled their noses, made rejecting noises round their teeth at putrid food; perhaps that was convention. There was something quite exciting about the smell of this chop, a powerful natural odour that might be as important as French perfume, or coffee, or violets. That might mean more in the scheme of things. She picked it up by its bone and looked at it. Would the cat like it? Ought she to give it to him? He should know whether it was right; could it be worse than a nearly dead bird, or warm mouse?

There was a pot of yoghurt at the back too, with several spoonfuls gone. Their place had been taken by a large flowering mould, that could be growing as she took the lid off and looked at it. It was mostly grey fur, long and silky like a silver fox, but some parts were a delicate rose pink, and there were some spots of a deep dark orange, an ancient colour, full of promise. And not just colours, pretty shapes as well, pleasing in their patterning. Would it continue to grow in the warmer kitchen, or did it need the cool dark fridge? Pity it should bloom unheeded there. She put it on the bench, beside the sink; she would see what happened.

The chop, the yoghurt: both in decay. She thought of the word, all her life the word decay. The decay of the west. Decayed ladies. Fight tooth decay. Decaying cavities. Releasing like the chop a secret shameful smell irresistible to the prying tongue. She boiled the jug and made a cup of tea, looking at the blooming yoghurt mould and wondering if all her life decay had tricked her—or was it that decay had been sadly tricked itself? A friend all along.

Change and decay in all around I see. She got the frying

pan and a slice of bacon. The left element of the stove was unusable; a great silver shape bulged sinuously through its coils; it looked like a diseased art nouveau pewter lily. What on earth's that, shrieked her daughters in turn. It was the bottom of a saucepan, one of the old aluminium saucepans she'd had since she was married. She'd forgotten the beans one day. You'll kill yourself Mum, they said. You could burn the house down, like that.

Change and decay in all around I see. She listened to the words in her head. They began to move up and down to their music. Once she'd have sung them, in her soft true voice that sang as a girl in her parents' house, as a bride in her own, as a mother, sang to grandchildren very quietly when her daughters weren't near, but now was stuck in her throat caught and thickened like the gargles of disgust. She saw the wooden vault of the church's roof polished dark and friendly. Nell's funeral, they'd sung the words at that. O thou who changest not, abide with me. Afterwards, three weeks later, they'd gone up to the headland and at the moment the sun set scattered her ashes into the sea below. Fast falls the eventide. The darkness deepens Lord with me abide. It was what she'd asked for, her ashes scattered. No children to piously observe her rosebush, and brothers and sisters nearing their own deaths. Maybe thinking of the expense. Who'd have thought a funeral so expensive. George had been cremated too, hated the thought of rotting in the earth, wanted it quick. She thought that being in the ground might be nice. Though after my skin worms destroy my body. She thought of lying in her grave and gradually sifting away. As people had always done, lying quiet. At rest. Peacefully returning to the earth from which we came. Pushing up daisies, people said. She liked daisies, their simple weedy faces. He cometh up, and is cut down, like a flower. Strewn on the gardener-fingered earth. None of the violence of the fire, the great roaring furnace, consuming everything. Too late now. The choices were made, the plot reserved. Beside George, sharing the same rosebush. Yellow. She'd only seen it in flower once, and that barely; the end of the season, one full-blown bloom, waiting to fall, age-speckled like her own skin, paper-frail. Other times every bush had been a skeleton, two or three short sticks, row upon row of thorny sticks. They do a great job of pruning, said her daughters, they must have marvellous flowers. Look, you can see where the new growth will come. But now they are cruel and thorny sticks, she said. Next time we'll come in the right season, they told her. Her and George, pushing up roses. Except they wouldn't be, the ashes were in a box, no flowers fed on them.

The bacon burnt. She heard it sizzling, smelt its black smell. She looked at it, tried to scrape it on to a plate, see if there were anything to be salvaged, but it had charred on to the bottom of the pan. She turned on the hot tap and held it under; there was a furious hiss, and clouds of steam, the pan buckled a bit more. She took it out to the compost. It wasn't a proper heap any more, just a hole in the ground. She gave it a few cuts with the spade, after all the rain it was rotting down nicely. Fifty years of saving scraps, the soil was rich with them. Crumbling friable vegetable-cossetting soil. She didn't grow anything now; daisies were spreading, and violets, and a rose-scented geranium creeping everywhere. The lawn, the grass, was six inches long, she'd have to get it cut. Lilies grew along the edge of the bank, you couldn't tell their spear-leaves from the grass. She thought that Josie, next door, whose garden was six feet lower, didn't like looking up at hers. It's a bit of a wilderness, she heard her say to her daughter. Alice liked wilderness but she didn't think Josie did. Maybe she thought

it was rather a burden on the yellow sandstone wall that held
it up. Maybe it devalued her property. The wilderness next door.
There were a couple of big trees, one was a eucalypt and the
ground around its base was covered with fallen leaves and twigs.
The woods decay . . . She scraped the bacon into the hole,
poked it down with the spade where the rats wouldn't find
it probably a bit black for them anyway and went inside. On
her dressing-table was a cut glass powder bowl with small oblongs
of newsprint in it. The woods decay, the woods decay and
fall. She'd cut them out of English *Women's Weeklys*, little verses
she liked the sound of. This was Tennyson. Man comes and
tills the fields and lies beneath. And after many a summer dies
the swan. That was nice. After many a summer. She thought
of Nell. She was a swan of many summers. They'd all swanned
through the summers once. Good summers they'd been. And
now her ashes were scattered on the sea. The tide frothing
and sucking as they'd so often watched it, the ashes swirling.
They'd have been dashed to pieces on the rocks now. Become
tiny minute fragments of the universe. Part of the lace-shredded
sea.

The tea had got pretty cold. She wouldn't have to wait until
it had cooled before she could drink it. She put some bread
in the toaster, and looked at the yoghurt mould. It seemed to
have got a bit bigger. There were purplish colours she hadn't
noticed before in little scatterings of spots. The orange, the purple,
the delicate rose-pink; they were rich colours, and varied, but
they went well together, they were harmonious against the silky
silver fox. Natural things could be full of colour and never clash.
Not like human ones.

What had happened to the toast? Still pale and cold. She'd
forgotten to turn the toaster on. She drank the tea and wondered
why people didn't grow mould gardens. A centrepiece for a

lunch party; put it in a little crystal bowl in the middle of the table. People eat blue cheeses, why not look at yoghurt mould gardens. The flavours of decay, and the beauty of it. Pleasing mouth and eye. It was a pity she never had people for lunch any more. She put margarine and vegemite on the toast and gave no thought to the bacon she'd intended to eat. Instead she watched the mould garden. She could imagine dress material with those colours, in those patterns, prettily water-colour sketched on silk, fine blue-white silk that would shimmer and quiver like yoghurt on a plate. The fabric cut with the sharp scissors never used for any other purpose, the skirt full on the bias and sleeves wide and gathered into narrow wrist-bands, the silk cool and soft against the skin, as yoghurt was, though silk not of course sloppy. She wondered where the scissors were. She could hear the powerful gobbling sound they made as they sliced through silk and sizzling taffeta and stiff shining cotton. She hadn't done any dressmaking for years. In the leather suitcase under the bed which she could hardly slide across the floor were scraps from the dresses she'd made in the past, and in the ottoman whose seat was a lid to be raised; all the bits of fabric which were a history of the lives of the women who'd worn the clothes they'd been made into; for those who had eyes to read. When she went her daughters would piece together the stories in part, but not completely. She should have called them in for a lesson. Here my girls is eighty years of dresses. Eighty years of the lives of the women who wore them. The dresses all gone now, become rags for dusting or washing cars, worn as draggled finery by little girls playing ladies, put into salvage bags for the Salvation Army or Vinny de Paul, ripped up for rag rugs. A while ago she'd begun to make patchwork, cutting the scraps of fabric into octagons and sewing them together in starry flowery patterns, and there the history could be read: your Sunday school dresses her christening robe the fifth year farewell Nell's seventieth birthday your wedding Min's golden anniversary the doll I made at the end of the war the square-dance skirt the ball gown the nightie the baby clothes the satin petticoat. All the meeting mating rituals and now the great grandchildren starting. George and Alice thinking only of themselves in love getting married coming together centred on their present, half a century ago now, and the generations spreading, multiplying. Patchwork quilts, family heirlooms because of the stories in them. But only if there are eyes to read and tongues to tell.

The Meals on Wheels lady saw the yoghurt mould garden and gargled disgust in her throat, ugh. I'd get rid of that if I were you love nasty poisonous thing. I think it's beautiful, she replied. I like to look at it. You could get sick things like that around said the woman clashing the metal dish cover. Lamb chop today nice and tasty it looks.

She didn't know about that. It was grey, and hard, like string compacted tight into a mass. The knife wouldn't go through it. She thought of her own old chop, decaying into lush pink tenderness, green as grouse at the table of a Lady. The cat had enjoyed it, called from the garden by the sweet green smell of its decay, tossing it about and growling at it as though it were a mouse, and now only the pared bone remained. She wondered what he'd make of this lump of impregnable damp matting.

In the night she woke up and lay in the dark listening to the sound of the cat lapping milk beside the bed. That was curious, because she never let the cat in at night; she fed him and shut him out on the verandah, where he could come and go through his own door. Even if he had tricked her and slipped back inside, there was no milk in the bedroom. Not even the dregs of her nightly Milo; the milk had boiled over and burnt in the saucepan and she hadn't bothered to start all over again. She listened, and then knew what it was. It was the clock ticking, sounding like a cat lapping milk beside the bed; every time she woke she heard it like that, though she knew what it was, the ticking clock sounding like a cat's tongue greedily lapping time. The clock was a gilt-faced alarm called Baby Ben; lying comfortable in bed in the dark she thought of her life as a shallow saucer that even a kitten could soon empty, lapping with its greedy tongue.

Beneficiaries

I am writing this with my mother's pen. She is slender, and very small, marbled green and brown and cream. I call it she because on top of the cap, which you have to fit on to the other end of the pen to make it long enough to write with, on this cap is a round ivory-coloured head, big-eyed, bobbed-haired, wearing a little flat black hat. Her face, with its two red spots for cheeks, has the knowing innocence of the twenties. Around her middle is a tarnished filigreed belt. Being a cylinder she has no waist, but that's the right shape for the period.

The nib has a slit in it, which ends in a hollow heart, and on it is written Peter Pan. The ink bag must have perished, it's no longer a fountain pen. You have to dip it into an ink bottle. I saw Elizabeth Jolley doing this in a movie about herself once. It's not much trouble, and lasts through a lot of words.

The letters flow in rich blue-black lines; the slender flapper who forms them writes with a bold spirit.

I wish I weren't using this pen. I've got it because my mother died. I've got my father's pen too. It's a stout navy blue job with a gold nib. A Parker. It somehow reminds me of Mr Menzies in a double-breasted suit. And of my father. He looked like Mr Menzies too, staying like him with those suits long out of fashion, but didn't like being told so because he couldn't stand his politics. You're the writer, Marion, my sisters said, you take the pens. I took a packet of post office nibs, too. Round Writer Pens, they're called. Please Note that our Celebrated Steel Pens bear our name in full, says the box. Who needs steel pen nibs now. I brought them because of school and my desire to be the ink monitor, filthy job, filling the china ink-wells every day, out of the bottle kept in the press. Remembering the great moment of stopping pencil writing and taking up pen.

Never think this doesn't work; voluptuously I trace the letters, and look, I've got my downstrokes back. Lightly up, then down so the steel nib splays and the ink ribbons out, the edges a fine dark selvedge to the fluid middle. I thought I'd lost the art. A handsome hand I'm writing here, though a bit scratchy. I feel like Mr Dickens. Moslem calligraphers say you need to learn to breathe, to get the rhythms of handwriting right, the dipping of the nib at the right moment. To suspend respiration in order to maintain the purity of the ink flowing. And the thinking following it, the contemplation of the next phrase beginning as the pen runs dry. I am being seduced by the rhythms of it. It's a Number 5 nib, quite thick I suppose. The holder—of course I brought a holder too—is very fat at the top, and tapering; it's red. I should think it's ergonomically very sound. Saving me from RSI. Sometimes at school people stabbed you with the sharp steel nibs. A hand in the wrong place, and stab! The inky blood flowing.

A mother dies, and there's a life to be divided up. Two lives; my father's things went on inhabiting the house after his death; books and music and a shed full of tools, the old double bed. Five even, if you count the three of us; we left home long ago, but we left our childhoods behind in the house, safely stored away should we ever need them.

The pens are easy. You take them, you're the writer, my sisters say. So is the organ, big solid wooden affair, with pedals; Annie's daughters will play it. Some things are kindly in threes: lamps, embroidered chairs, monumental vases. The linen is no problem; we shuffle it out, like a deck of cards. A duchess set for you, for you, for you; a round of doyleys, another, another. A few hands of teatowels. We know the provenance of these: the holiday in Tasmania, the trip overseas, the visits to daughters, the presents sent by them: King's College Cambridge, the cities of New Zealand, Culpeper's herbs. Sheets are easily divisible, and blankets. The treasures are balanced and bartered: the great damask linen tablecloths (you can have the stags), the teacloths embroidered for a glory box fifty years and more ago, the deeply crusted crochet coming maybe from the wedding a generation before that; we recognise our grandmother's handiwork. Bea and I won't let Annie have the cutlery or the silver-traced dinner set; she'll put them in the dishwasher and wreck them. I wouldn't, I just wouldn't ever use them; Bea is safe, she hasn't got a dishwasher. Annie can have the sofa bed instead.

I take the dining-table, hideous mock wood laminex, with leaves that pull out and legs that screw off. Father bought it for my twenty-first birthday party, by telephone, from work. I don't think my mother ever forgave him. Such an important purchase not to be chosen by long searching, examination, comparison. But it fitted great family parties, parents, three daughters, three sons-in-law, seven grandchildren. No, never that many. Father died two days after the last child was born; we told him, but nobody knew whether he took it in or not. He'd have thought it fitting, a death and a life together. Fourteen we were at table, often, but never fifteen.

Even the fridge and the telly and the washing machine are no problem; we, the Beneficiaries, agree quite happily on those. The Beneficiaries, that's what the Public Trustee calls us, turning us into figures on a legal document, above-mentioned, aforesaid, here noted, undersigned. We won't be like our aunts, and fall out. (A teacup, that's all I got. Not bone china either. And I was married to the eldest son, even if he did die thirty years ago.) We're blood sisters, no in-laws, no brothers' wives, to feel done down by daughters sure their mother's things belong to them and not to relations by marriage. Interlopers without the gift of needlework.

We go through the clothes. Our mother never threw anything away. Years of clothes are there. Bea picks up a limp rolled bundle, shakes it out. It's a dress of voile, thin enough to strain cheese through, pale white patterned with paisley commas that might have been painted in blue ink. Round-necked, small-waisted. Bea holds it against her body as though she were thinking of buying it. Remember how pretty she looked in this? We can all see her. Off to the Alcron for cousin Peter's twenty-first. With a rhinestone brooch and a new perm. It's more than twenty years ago, just when we were all off her hands, and father not yet retired. Her life was her own, for a while; the hard work and hand-me-downs were in the past, and she bloomed. There are richly fabricked dresses from this time, silk taffetas and gorgeous brocades like contour maps of busy landscapes, for weddings and wearing to dinner on Orsova, when they went on their world tour. Their bus trip to Scotland chose her to play the bride at Gretna Green, because she was the prettiest father said; she had her photo taken in the veil kept there for the purpose; the cream linen suit is her own and so is that look in the eye the best brides have, a look that gazes on happiness ahead.

None of the clothes fit us. Even at her plumpest, our mother was smaller than her strapping daughters. Seven stone nothing when I married her, father used to say. When we were small she was thin, worn ragged was his expression. Then there was that second blooming, and later she became a plump little granny. When she died she weighed thirty-one kilos, a frail parcel of bones in worn flesh, looking out at the world with the big observing thinking eyes of a child.

Bea tries on a silk dress, she's the slightest, but it's too small, too short. She finds an old ball dress of hers; it still fits her. That's because Mum made it too loose, she says. Remember how she'd never make things tight enough?

We fold everything up, sort it into good quality and raggy. There are a lot of shoes, some hardly worn, from when she still bought pretty shoes though her feet wanted comfortable flat lace-ups for all the walking she still did. All too tiny for our big feet. In the dressing-table drawers, stuffed at the back, Annie keeps finding bras. Each time she pulls one out we giggle, until finally we're sitting in this pile of lacy skin-coloured engineering garments, helpless with laughter. There must be two dozen, says Bea. Every time she went shopping she must've bought a bra. She had an extravagant idea of her size. They're not worn. Annie and I try some of them on. They give us pointy bosoms like fifties sweater girls. We're laughing so much we're crying, we can hardly see ourselves. What can she have been thinking of, says Bea. Annie and I wear the bras for the rest of the week. Every time we notice our noble shapes, the laughter wells up again.

I keep the blue and white voile. I remember when she bought the material, when she and father were visiting me; I bought some too, in brown and white, to make a maternity dress. That pregnancy was the first grandchild, twenty-two years ago now. It was a rather hopeless maternity dress, too transparent; hers worked much better.

We ring up the Smith Family about the clothes. Yes, they'll be open. But when we get there they aren't. There's a big bin outside. I want to come back tomorrow and hand over the things, explain in words what they are, but Annie says we haven't got time. We stuff all the plastic bags through the slit in the bin, hear them fall plop. I feel as though I am stuffing my mother in the bin.

We had no choice, says Annie. There's still so much to do. Time's running out. She's right of course.

At night we make little dinners and drink red wine out of a cask. We've never lived together before. I left home when Annie was fourteen. In those days we all fought. The night of the clothes in the bin we have a fight, not over things, it's because we're upset over this vast demolition job we've only got a week to do. Our children and our husbands and our careers in other cities can't do without us any longer than that. It's one of those fights nobody can remember the start of. We have another glass of wine and go through papers. Fifty years and never anything thrown away. Bills and cuttings and Christmas cards, wedding invitations, birth notices, lay-by slips. They're documents, says Bea. They're part of history. It's a crime to throw them away. But what can we do? We keep the photographs, to sort through another day. And letters. There's one written by our mother to her childhood friend, Addie she went to school with, wishing her a happy birthday. It begins: *As little girls we did not think we would be eighty some day.* It was never posted. Addie's dead now too . . .

What about the knitting patterns? The recipes? Some of them date back to the forties. Valuable social data. To be preserved. We're our mother's daughters. Maybe the National Library?

It's too hard to organise. Out they go, into the bright green hopper marked Clean Valley we've had delivered. By a handsome young man in white overalls who chats us up. You sisters? he says. For a minute we're the girls we once were in this house.

We discover that our mother kept diaries. All her life. There are gaps, and most entries are brief, but all her life she wrote it down. *May 8th 1977. Went to the Louvre. Marion got the washing dry.* She's summed it up exactly, says Annie. That's just what it's like being overseas. Going to the Louvre and getting the washing dry.

In our diaries we'd only have written down the Louvre, and that would have been only half the picture. She's written down all the ordinary bits. Listen to this, we say to one another, flipping pages:

Had my hair permed. Mrs Thompson gave me some lemons.

Rained and I sewed.

Jamie and I had a picnic to the blackberry patch. Lovely day got my face burned red. Picked five pounds blackberries, made 2 tarts and some jam.

Finished reading The Admirable Crichton.

Marion flew up from Canberra looking very well. Not surprising, I say. I was twenty-four that year.

Annie and I went to town and bought first grapes. Bea came for Dinner. We had chicken and apple crumble.

That's when I was living in that flat, says Bea. Before I got married.

Ninety degrees in dining-room today.

Oh look. *Leaving results today.* That's you Annie. Annie's results. *Second . . .*

Annie grabs the book. *Washing machine man came and went and didn't come back.* Typical. Some things never change.

Fire in the paddock at the back. I remember that, says Annie. The fire brigade came.

Made a chocolate cake. Helped paint the fence a little.

Went to mother's in the afternoon. Lou had gone to town with the hearing aid so we could not converse very much.

Bought a nice cream felt hat. Took Jamie to show his approval and he liked it.

Burning paint off was Jamie. She obviously got a bit bored with the paint burning off; it goes on for pages.

We could spend forever on this. All work has stopped. There's just the diaries, us reciting lines at one another, like a litany.

Peter had a party at his flat.

Annie very poorly today after last night's party. Hmm, grins Bea. She's not too impressed, is she?

The stocks in the garden just now are beautiful, very colourful.

Dad's birthday. A shirt each from three daughters. We all laugh. Imagine what he'd've said, says Annie.

Bea peers over Annie's shoulder. That's a full day, she says. It's your wedding day, says Annie.

There it is, all the detail. All that daily data we never think to remember, and suddenly we feel ourselves as we were then, as the westerlies blew and the Christmas puddings boiled, and the stocks scented the sea-breeze evenings.

These precious documents we put into a wooden deed box. I'm the eldest, I'm to be custodian.

It's stopped being easy, but it's going well. The Beneficiaries are still excellent friends. The jewellery's divided, a bit sad the jewellery, none of it worth much, except the rings, and they're the only belongings she portioned out beforehand, the diamonds to Bea and me, the amethyst to Annie. The glassware's done, and the kitchenware—most of this St Vinny's stuff. The house is still full. The week's nearly up, and still so much to do. Now we discover the really hard part. We sit on the hard wooden dining chairs, stretching our aching backs, and gaze helplessly at loaded surfaces.

That's nice, Annie, why don't you have it.

Oh no, I don't need that. I've got two already.

Bea?

I don't know what to do with all the stuff I've got. I don't need any more. You have it.

But I don't really want it either.

We can't throw it away.

It's terribly hideous.

It was a wedding present.

It's not worth much.

Oh, I don't know. It's rather nice.

You have it then.

I don't need it.

Who needs anything?

Put it in the Vinny's box.

Can't do that.

Take it for the kids.

They won't want it.

Mum was really fond of that.

You're just being sentimental.

I remember when they bought it. How thrilled they were.

Somebody's got to have it.

I need to throw my junk away. Not collect more.

Twenties sheet music, half a dozen hymn books, tomes of military biography, Murano glass, early LPs of Tchaikovsky and Welsh choirs, patchwork stuffs, cut glass honey pots, clocks that could be got to work, painted cake plates, biscuit tins, taffeta sofa cushions, souvenirs of South Africa in carved black wood . . . They need the eyes of their owners to make them desirable.

No problem sharing out the things we liked and wanted; our apportioning was scrupulously fair. Each of us gave up something we liked, each of us offered not to take things, pressed goodies on the others. We are sisters as well as Beneficiaries, we said to one another, we will remain friends and not fall out over objects. But this is defeating us. All these things that our parents valued, saved for, treasured, and none of us wants them. Each wants the others to take them, no one wants the responsibility or the guilt of disposing of them. This is where the battle of wills begins. This is where we fall out, over the things we don't want.

We order the carriers, three to go our separate distant ways. We've sold, we've thrown away, we've given, we've kept. We suspect we've kept the wrong things, thrown away what we should have hung on to. I look now about my house, at the odd things I don't really care for, that my conscience stopped me chucking. I'm glad, I suppose, though they do litter the place rather. This cake plate, for instance, green as a mantled pond, with a chrome stem that screws in the middle and has a twig of green—what: bakelite? nally ware?—forming a handle on the top. Great stuff if you're into kitsch. And the pink china lady with yellow bobbed hair (big sister of the pen) who dances amid a solid frou-frou of skirts. The cobalt blue wall plaque, with its yellow-sailed windmill and pink and green peach-blossom; maybe I'll hang it in the spare room, one of these days. It was a wedding present, one of the few that survived us kids; it's only got a hairline crack.

One thing went. There were rubber stamps with my father's name, one in flowing script, another printed. We said, no use now, there is no one of this name, never will be, and threw them in the big green hopper.

So the house is stripped bare, except for a mirror on the wall. It hasn't looked like this for forty-five years. It's open, and somehow fresh looking. This is a new start for it; the man and the woman (she looks about fifteen) who will pay a good price at auction will paint it and polish the floors and it will be again the house of a young married couple having children. Who will love the minute-away beach as we did, and catch the bus to town, and go to Junction School. My mother and grandmother went to Junction School, too. It was 125 years old the other day.

And I'm an orphan, and the head of the family. And my childhood is no longer there in that house for me whenever I want it. At least its new owners aren't going to pull it down and build flats, as happens round here. And I'm sure they'll be grateful for the trees I gave my parents the Christmas I was eighteen. Such tall and shady trees are rare so near the sea. Pohutekawa they are, New Zealand Christmas Bush, tough-leaved and scarlet-flowered, able to flourish through salty gales. I went to a nursery and found that out.

The pen blots. That's the trouble with dipping in inkwells. Messy business. And needing more skill than you remember.

Salut,
Dr Appleton

*W*hen I went to university, and in the town I went to university in, people still debated the desirability of higher education for women. Whether it was a waste of time and money and effort, since girls just got married, and there you were, years of training down the drain. A bunch of squalling brats, same as any other woman.

You shouldn't assume from this that I'm 110, either. Would you believe forty—or so. Of course, we're not talking about one of your great universities (it was in fact three years old, and a college of somewhere else) or the daughters of the middle class. Anyway, all things considered, it was amazing that I talked myself into a tertiary education, given all the *données* of the situation. But a good Leaving Certificate pass helped, and so did my parents' very sensible perception that I wouldn't be happy unless I got it; they might have been ignorant but they weren't unkind. So they did their best to ignore the sideways disapproval of the relations, though they couldn't always stop themselves wondering where it was all going to lead: philosophy, French, even history; what possible relevance could they have to people like us, in a town like that, in this country?

The thing was, it didn't seem to occur to anybody to consider that there was more than the ostensible curriculum involved. Fair enough, for my backward relations. But the lecturing staff could have made the point rather better.

Only one at all tried. And must have despaired of success. But this is wisdom after the event. At the time we saw absurdity, which we didn't always dignify with the title of eccentricity; it is the passing years that have shown affection. And so now I feel like calling him 'my old professor', or even, claiming intimacy, 'my old prof', though at the time I knew him he was simply Head of Department (and for a while, Department as well) in a newborn university college of a grubby old seaside industrial town. Later both he and college achieved the honour of establishment, and he became a real professor in a real university. Did it add even more to his dignity, I've always wondered; it's hard to imagine any augmentation of that severe and scholarly presence. Anyway, calling him my old prof can only have a youthening effect, and since age is a figment of other people's imaginations, why not?

I was late for his first class, inadvertently but that was irrelevant. I'd misjudged the time it took to walk from the bus a mile or two. I hurried, even ran most of the time, past the used car lots silently screaming unbeatable bargains in guanos of strident chalk all over other people's cast-offs, past their thousands of little flags grimly fluttering in the salty industrial breeze. Along under the almost immemorial fig-trees, improbably huge, dropping their sticky inedible fruit and scenting the air with a pleasing faint rottenness. Across the creek, the muddy relic of a storm water drain now the tide was out, and up the drive to arrive streaming and twitching in so much heat in the tiny but towering seminar room where Doctor Appleton had already produced enough impeccable monotonous French to flatten twelve downcast students.

I wasn't even very late, it was just that nobody had told me he always started five minutes early. And in French, which was doubly shattering. Nobody had told me that, either, and it was difficult to see how we were going to learn much if it was taught to us in its own almost incomprehensible language. Five years of studying it at school hadn't actually warned us against the possibility of having to understand people speaking it.

The seminar room was high-ceilinged as a big lecture hall, but only about ten feet square, and windowless; the measured flow of French was caught and held by it like liquid filling a jar, and I sat drowning in it and my own rivers of sweat as the blood pumped too fast through my veins and my skin throbbed with a knowledge of irretrievable error, the sin of lateness lost in the horror of having chosen the wrong subject, a career ruined and all my beautiful hopes blighted.

Then I began to understand it was a matter of overweening. It was all very well to be clever, the successful product of a selective state school, but when it came to going to university, it was obvious that origins would out. The working class: what did it have to do with higher education? For a female at that. One's family and acquaintances were absolutely right in their suspicions, their sinister gleeful expectation of sticky ends, based on the most percipient of reasonings: nobody had done it before, people like us didn't, what good could come of it. They didn't know the word, but I did, having been happily immured in an ivory tower for the past five years: it was *hubris*. And the punishment would be inescapable, now as in ancient times.

Well, it wasn't as bad as that, of course. That turned out to be Dr Appleton's annual inaugural student scaring lecture. After it classes proceeded rationally and properly in English, and I had learned not to be late. I caught the bus half an hour earlier, and the worst thing that happened was my meeting him sometimes in the corridor, his gold rococo clock held far in front of him, like a lantern in a dark waste, by thumb and finger looped together through its curlicue of a handle, its elegant scrolled face turned outwards, as though it were carried as a reproach to the world rather than as a timekeeper for its owner. At such times he stood back against the wall in a courtly but unseeing gesture, so that one entered the room before him, technically at least on time.

We never dared be late with proses, either. He'd warned us with a cautionary tale of *his* old prof, who once on his way to collect the weekly batch of exercises met a student, running through the snow, five minutes late with his exercise. 'I'm terribly sorry, sir,' gasped the boy. 'I'm afraid I'm late. My mother died this morning.'

'Nevertheless, my boy,' replied the old man gently, 'I'm afraid I cannot accept it. Punctuality is only a virtue if practised under all circumstances.'

Nobody was quite sure whether Dr Appleton would have been so strict, since nobody in his three years of rule—already the tradition was building up—had dared to try him. But I did find out later that he'd been a pupil of the great Professor N—at Sydney. Hurrying through the snow, in Sydney?

The little gold clock, frivolous in demeanour perhaps, but with the basic seriousness of all time-telling machines, stood on his desk all lesson; exactly on the hour he picked up his books and departed, clock again before him, lighting his way back along the dim ugly corridor to his own room. And when we made particularly bad mistakes in proses—like failing to make verb and subject agree, or putting the wrong gender, or an improper preposition—then he didn't just cross it out, he drew a picture frame around it, which one knew was an elaborate gilt picture frame even though it was drawn in red ink, and its elegant rococo curls recalled the pretty lines of the little French clock. It was a very complete picture frame, right up to a thin string and a nail to hang it on. Dr Appleton stood in front of us and smiled the small self-conscious smile that always preceded a joke. 'We have . . . quite . . . a number . . . of works . . . of art, today.'

Naturally it was not a good thing to have many of these, people tried hard to avoid them. One could tell at a glance a good prose by their absence; a page at all decorated with such Royal Academy recognition was almost certainly a failure. Everybody in the class peered at everybody else's work, looking for gilt—the first time I wrote guilt—picture frames in red ink.

I made quite a collection of these frames, in all their subtle variation. I didn't seem able to avoid silly mistakes. And my pronunciation wasn't good either. My friend Sally was in the same position; Dr Appleton said we must come for extra tuition, and it would have to be at 8 o'clock in the morning because Sally was a part-time student and worked from nine till five.

It was quite hard work getting there on the cold winter mornings of second term, but I don't think we minded it much. At least I got up with the rest of the family and avoided any criticism of idle lie-abed university students when were they going to get some real work done. We weren't absolutely punctual, the filigreed gold hands usually said a little after eight, but Dr Appleton didn't seem to accuse. My pronunciation improved a bit, Sally's a lot. We learned to make a proper *i* sound, and worked hard on a French *u*.

'Stretch your lips back and set your tongue and teeth as though you were saying *eee*,' he'd say, his fact split in a tense and mirthless grin. 'Say it, say *eee*.'

'*Eee*,' we would say.

'Good. Now leave tongue and teeth exactly as they are but push your lips forward as in *ooo*.' And his lips would funnel forward, and out would come a perfect French *u*.

Sometimes we managed it. Sometimes his thick grey hair would shake and his eyes half close, and then we'd pass on to the next thing. And precisely at fifteen minutes to nine he'd show us out with an unsmiling correct bow, and Sally would race off to work, and I would go and wait for the library to open, and be with any luck first in the queue for the big Harrap's dictionary, which was the only thing to use if you wanted good marks in proses.

Occasionally I met him in the street, walking firmly along under the fig trees, and he never spoke or acknowledged my presence, and even in the corridors of the university he was equally remote, never going beyond an exaggerated withdrawal to one side, with a sharpish slight nod that might have been a bow, might have been irritation. Once I stopped to ask him about some books; he ordered copies of texts from Paris for us because it was cheaper and quicker that way. (These books were a trap for lazy students; if you hadn't prepared your work it was made obvious by your having to cut the pages in class. Ripping them surreptitiously made shrill little reports in the pellucid silence of the lesson.) While I spoke he edged away, and as soon as I had finished he rushed off. His retreating back made me feel like a fury he was escaping from.

He was an excellent subject for us to practise our newly

found psychology on. (Most of us used a psych unit to fill a gap in our degrees and made much use of the jargon.) We knew he lived alone in a rather seedy hotel whose grandeur was decaying along with its unfashionable end of town, up near the beach, and had his dinner always at the same respectable cafe. He was never seen to speak to anybody at all.

And yet in his own room or in class he was urbane, sweetly smiling, full of little jibes of wit at our expense or that of the authors we were reading. He made elegant and formal translations of these; sometimes he pretended he wanted our help in thinking up a word which would exactly give the feeling of the French, but it was only so that he could come out the more triumphantly with the word that he'd had in his own head all the time. 'Nautch girls' was one such; he seemed surprised that we hadn't heard of it, but gently insisted that we use it. We rather despised it as a euphemism for what was already a euphemism anyway, but I did look it up and found out it was a perfectly useful word, even if it does come from Hindu. It means dancing girls. Browning used it, so it was probably a good thing to graft it on to Hugo.

He was certainly justified in not having much faith in the general cultivation of a motley collection of first-year students in a new university college. Anybody with any money or pretension went away, to Sydney or Armidale. Some of us were kids straight from school, seventeen or like me only sixteen, some were part-time students, most were female, all after that doubtfully valid higher education. Clever enough, but unformed. And yet he never let us see how unprepossessing we must have been. Instead he tried to raise our general level of culture, with a French bias of course; he arranged films for us, and exhibitions of books and prints and photographs. He'd provide music with them, and sit dreamily playing Edith Piaf and Charles Trenet and Jacques Brel at the tops of their voices. I was shocked; I'd been brought up by a piano-playing father to despise pop music, and this often noisy raucous stuff with its throbbing powerful beat was just the sort of fearful racket I'd been led to believe was totally foreign to the nature of true music. Yet here was this serious austere person obviously enjoying its vulgarities. It was probably one of the more useful shocks of my university career.

◆　◆　◆

Sally was tall and delicate with pale hair looped at the back of her neck and that plain serious beauty that always makes one think of the unfleshly images of Virgins. The grey bank uniform suited her very well in its long neat fashion; the mini skirt that has left bank uniforms permanently abbreviated (why always above such fat thighs?) had not yet arrived on the scene. Dr Appleton took special care with Sally's pronunciation, lovingly sketching out the dreadful grimaces that would produce the right sounds. He took less trouble with me; I assumed that he saw at once that I was fairly hopeless.

'Dr Appleton is in love with you, you know,' said Jill to her after class one day. Jill was a bit older than us, with already a degree and a job as a dietician. She was doing French to keep from stagnating.

Sally was annoyed. 'That's silly,' she said. 'Of course he couldn't possibly be.'

I wondered, watching him earnestly regarding her soft face, her large grey eyes, Sally leaning gracefully and anxiously towards him and he drawing the precise sounds from her lips as though she were an opera singer producing perfect notes. He did like looking at her. But in love with her?

We saw less of Jill as it became obvious that she was seeing more of Marc Amiot, a lively tutor just arrived that year from France, and giving Dr Appleton a Department to be Head of. I never knew whether she had inside knowledge of Dr Appleton's emotions or whether she had the lover's tendency to see everyone else in the same situation. When she got engaged to Marc in third term she invited us to the party, held in her parents' enormous house and garden. Jill had done her first degree at Sydney University, and knew how to give an elegant party. There were throngs of interesting people, including lots of faculty members, and of course the French department. By the end of the evening the amazing Dr Appleton was sitting on a dimly lit verandah surrounded by a small crowd of people who shouted with laughter every few minutes. It seemed he was telling anecdotes, very funny ones; I was too shy to go close enough to find out. Fancy the old prof as the life and soul of a party. It was a momentous evening for me; I ate my first olive, and hated it; quite unprophetically.

'I have to call him Henry now,' said Jill. It was difficult to think of Dr Appleton's having a Christian name, and how could she call him by it? But after that we all did. As a nickname. Only Jill ever used it to his face.

'Henry' had insisted we join the *Alliance Française*, out of that general concern for our culture; most thankless of tasks, one would have thought. He never gave up trying to make us see that French was a language that worked in the world, not just difficult poems and rotund prose, but a means of vulgar communication. But it had to be created rather artificially in our fine philistine city, where people thought you were mad to be learning a language there wasn't the remotest chance of your ever getting to speak on its native soil. There wasn't much of a French community around to give the *Alliance* a solid basis, but it flourished in its own way, with films and lectures and visits from the French merchant navy; they involved cocktail parties on tidy white boats and provided a snobbish reason for joining. Its most ambitious project of the year was a dinner, to be held at Beau Vista, an Edwardian villa fashionable for wedding receptions. There were to be three courses, with suitable wines.

Sally and I went, in some trepidation at this excursion into high life, but none the less feeling we were finding our true milieu at last. We didn't tell our parents about the wine, assuming in them a working-class ignorance of civilised drinking. They'd have seen it as a first step on the primrose path. As we did ourselves, in fact, but we knew we could handle it. We would just sip it, taste it, for the experience, and not drink it, thus preserving our Methodist teetotalitarianism, at the same time as becoming acquainted with the finer things of life. And after all, we would have paid for it, it was properly ours, we had a right to it.

Sally wore a very plain dark red dress that made her look stunningly beautiful; I wore a rather pretty outfit that did little for me: an unfortunate habit that the years have done little to redress. The rooms of Beau Vista were warm, glowing, rich, the people full of social graces. They circulated, talked, laughed; we didn't know how to manage it. None of our fellow students seemed to have come, presumably less avid for all the delights of a cultured life than Sally and I. Except Jill, of course, who was lost in the centre of a small group of rapidly chattering French people. Being engaged to Marc seemed to be doing wonders for her French. Dr Appleton moved about the room, his hands clasped behind his back, inclining his body slightly forward so that it was ever ready for the formal little bow, the sweet smile whose self-consciousness caused his eyes to close and him to move on to the next person. For a while he stood in a large bay window, looking at the lights of the city.

Sally and I had tried that for a bit. Then she had sat us down on a stuffed red velvet bench in front of a coffee table with books on it, and together we looked rather animatedly at a large volume of black and white photographs of French cathedrals. After a while Dr Appleton came past, and stood before the table, smiling that enigmatic smile of a kindly uncle about to give one a lovely present with which he pretended to think up just the precise translation of a difficult word. He bent towards us, twirled his fingers in maestro fashion, and said:

'Say *u!*'

We laughed properly, he went away. It was a relief when we went in to dinner.

The first course was *pâté*. 'It's a kind of meat loaf,' said Sally, who distrusted all butcher's mince. It was served with white wine; the waiters came with bottles.

'Are you taking wine, madame?'

'Yes please.'

We took a sip, cautiously. It tasted thin, a bit bitter. It was easy not to drink any more.

The next course was *coq au vin*; the waiter brought red wine. He looked at our full glasses, and almost passed by, but said, formally:

'*Red* wine, madame?'

'Yes please.'

The red was thicker, it felt more potent. The horrors of strong drink fumed up more headily from that glass.

'It tastes like cough mixture,' said Sally. 'Fancy drinking a whole glass of the stuff.'

Plenty of people were, and even more than one. We'd never really seen people drinking before. Dr Appleton just down the table sipped and sipped, feeling the wine in his mouth. When he saw me looking at him, he raised his glass a little, bowed, and drank. It was confusing: should I do the same? I only smiled, and looked away. The waiters came several times and filled glasses; we regarded their owners. Perhaps they were getting drunk; perhaps they'd become like the people one saw stumbling and vomiting outside hotels when they closed at six o'clock.

The last course was chocolate cake, rich and rummy, respectable enough—since alcohol in cakes was quite proper and indeed bottles of sherry were kept in wowser households for that purpose—and much more comfortable, since though we'd said the *coq au vin* was delicious, it was a little bizarre, not the sort of thing one was used to at all. I've often wondered what that meal was really like; I suspect it probably wasn't very good, would not at all impress me now, but I can't possibly tell. The waiter at least was very smooth. The cake was served with muscat (it was indeed, an Australian French meal); again he eyed the two full glasses, again inquired:

'Some sweet wine, madame?'

'Yes please.'

The muscat was altogether more seductive, one could imagine drinking that. All the more reason for being strong; there is only virtue in resisting temptation when it is difficult. The third full glass took its place beside the others. Perhaps people were looking askance at this somewhat eccentric behaviour, or perhaps they were feeling irritated at the wastage of wine that they could have imbibed themselves. Too bad. We could do what we liked with our own.

'Gosh,' said Sally. 'Just a sip makes you feel light-headed. It's really strong.'

'I hope my mother doesn't smell my breath when I get home.'

'Oh dear. I never thought of that. My mother'll kill me.'

'Am I imagining it, or are people getting redder looking?'

'Redder, I think. And noisier. And listen to the laughing.'

Voices were rising and falling, chairs were pushing back
to make conversational curves around the table. Dr Appleton,
his aged planet's face dimpled and crinkling round the eyes,
had his companion hanging on his words. He seemed to be
telling a funny story about the little *pensione* in Rome where
he always stayed. Though a French scholar he was impassioned
of Italy, and often told us so. Jill and Marc looked into one
another's eyes and toasted themselves sensuously in muscat;
the French of their friends became gayer and sharper and even
more of a foreign language. Sally and I sat and sipped our coffee
and dissected our first formal dinner, and decided it was really
very nice, though not so glamorous as we'd expected, and not
as exciting.

What a pair of foul little prigs we were. Now as I grow
plumper and pinker, with the little red veins bursting in my
cheeks—oh madame, your capillaries!—I remember those three
only tasted glasses of wine, the tall and yellow, the round and
red, the small and brown, with a great deal of horror for the
meanness—of spirit, not purse—that lined them up, all exacted
as paid for, and did not see that they might have been enjoyed.
How contemptible was our virtue. Those three full glasses were
the most offensive of gestures, never mind the excuse of our
youth. Now I blush (or perhaps flush, vinously) for the ugly
pride of sobriety that sustained us through that evening in an
intoxication more deceptive than the wine could have produced.
But I have expiated the sin since; I look back upon a long
line of wine glasses, all emptied, most enjoyed. I just wished
I'd emptied one of them returning Dr Appleton's toast that night.

I suppose it's some consolation that I've done so since; well,
metaphorically. The year ended, Sally's with a credit, mine with
a pass, barely deserved, and I dropped French. Got out while
the going was good, you might have said. But the funny thing

is I still speak it, quite often, with a dreadful accent (I've lost any small skill I had with the old shibboleth *u*) and using only the present and occasionally the perfect tenses. I once tried to explain that the great herring runs—the current one of which had furnished the fish cooked in white wine with bay leaves we were at that moment eating, served by me at a dinner party in Paris to some sympathetic French friends—that these herring runs were immemorial, exploited by stone age as well as twentieth century man. I tried to explain it in the present tense. It rather ruined the whole fascinating observation. How Dr Appleton would have laughed. Or shuddered. But he'd have enjoyed the food, the delicately flavoured peasanty herring, and the altogether more aristocratic Muscadet de Sèvre et Maine we drank with it. *Salut*, Dr Appleton.

it. Salut, Dr Appleton.

Vale,
Professor
Appleton

*T*hat first story about Dr
Appleton: I wrote it out of a kind of modesty; innocence even;
ignorance. (How pejorative am I going to let the words get?)
The modesty I can explain. I didn't really think of the story's
being read. I wrote it, yes, with all the care and skill I could
muster then, I knew I was doing it, was quite consciously turning
those facts into my fiction, but I didn't actually think of anybody
reading it. A failure of the imagination, you might say. Because
I sent it off, hoping it would be published, and it was, though
not instantly, but I followed it no further, did not picture any
of those readers, you readers—for I know you're there, now—
who have turned fiction back into fact.

I suppose a lot of new writers are like this. They write for
the sake of writing. It takes a while to learn the logic of the
next step, the *I write, I publish, therefore I am read* proposition.

Look at all the Is on this page. You don't see them as I do, the inky loop blue-black on the milk-blue surface, the tail curving down, not touching the line, curling up, bouncing along, quite different from any other capital letters; come to think of it, there are no other capital letters, well hardly, just these bouncy insouciant Is, meaning to apologise maybe, but do they? They in fact just go on in the same old way, compounding the original—well, I suppose it's not a crime, really, writing stories about old teachers.

You—I'm imagining you, reader, now that I know you're out there—to you the Is don't look like this, they're upright black bars on a printed page; much more severe, military even. That private inky I: a drop of water and it'll run, and there's only one copy of the paper, easily lost; just now it blew off the table in my absence and I couldn't find it (you in turn can picture me losing my temper in my untidy room with the green summer treetops crowding outside), blamed gremlins, poltergeists, scared by this intimation of frailty; that I who was me then didn't imagine these organised print Is, so many of them, all falling into different hands, all read. What I did know, though—I the person, myself, not the sign on the page—must have known since I acted on it so thoroughly, though doubtless not admitting then, is that writers are vampires, are cannibals, are carrion feeders on anything whose life so much as shimmers within the ambit of their eyes. Whose life . . . yes . . . and death too if it makes a good story.

Hubris, you might call it, that overweening myself-as-centre-of-the-universe and all is grist to my mill stuff. The narrator of my story suspects herself of it and that in itself is a kind of hubris. I am less brave; I insist it was modesty that allowed me so blatantly to turn another's life into a story. It was there to be done, I did it. And then was surprised to discover people reading my account of the professor of French, a man of comical courtliness and passionate scholarship, in a new university on a creek-canal in a grotty industrial town by the sea, trying to educate a bunch of kids, clever enough but as shapeless and ignorant as the institution that had to be invented too. Trying to instil in us his love of a foreign language, its strictness, and to make us believe in the new life it offered. I described him walking down dingy corridors, 'his gold rococo clock held far in front of him, like a lantern in a dark waste'. Returning proses with more of his red ink on them than our blue, red ink that turned into gilt picture frames around basic errors. And then the story was quoted in his obituary. Called *a not-too-heavily-veiled tribute. Which well captures the affection felt for him by students and colleagues and also chronicles some of his more egregious quirks and oddities.*

Come on, I said, it's fiction. Who do you think you're kidding, said Cosmo.

The question is, did *he* read it? That didn't occur to me at the time. The university archivist, who must keep whatever records he can however unlikely, and confesses to not being in the habit of reading fiction but enjoying this one, the archivist suspects he did, that he was glad, that one of the reasons for the bequest was the tiny grain of love that he could have found in my story. Though I had spared him nothing: the seedy hotel, the ageing planet's face, the absurdity not always recognised as eccentricity. The cold clever eye of the student, of the grim *them* that a teacher must always face, transposing into the merciless artificer of fictions. Still, there was a perception of what his endeavours were about, a faint adumbration of gratitude. Culture was what I saw he wanted for us, and culture I suppose is what I was practising, since publishing stories in literary magazines must be a classical unprofitable version of it.

Everyone who knew Dr Appleton, Professor he became after my time, made a story out of him. The obituary mentions this. The canon, it calls it. Everybody having a favourite, and where old students and colleagues met, vying with one another to produce the most bizarre, outlandish, comical. The taking of a girl to the zoo, in 1939, and showing her a female monkey masturbating. Expecting to have a conversation about it. Being surprised when she ran away. The claim that he was on first name terms with every prostitute in King's Cross. For as well as other people's stories about him, there were the stories he made of himself. He offered his life as a series of eccentric anecdotes, which preserved his mystery inviolate. And his death . . . his death is his own narrative as well. Shapely, classical, ironic.

It begins with his retirement. That other story, the one written by the nameless undazzling student of French in the grubby industrial town by the sea; if you want to read it you'll have to look it up. 'Salut, Dr Appleton' it's called. *Southerly*, 4, 1982. December. Page 387. I wasn't, as I say, offering it as fact. The meal, for instance, the *Alliance Française* dinner, I think I remember the wines, and perhaps the *pâte*, but the other courses . . . not a clue. I made them up. I think I did. Though maybe what I made up was what we actually ate. Who knows. And the story about the pension in Rome; it was what seemed likely, that's all.

Then there's the prose. I'm not entirely happy about it. I mean if I were writing it now I'd do it differently. In places. More sparely, probably. The old less-is-more. The last paragraph is clumsy, I knew from the beginning, I wrote it over and over. The trouble is I wanted to mention the herring runs before the meal, the one in Paris, and then put in the last bit, how I talked about stone age man in the present tense. But it is clumsy. I could rewrite it now, but can you go on forever rewriting the fictions of the past?

I always use the present tense when I speak French. For grammatical reasons, I've even less control of the others. The story telling tense: see it happening now. Immemorial herring run, stone age people feeding off you, here you are, this minute.

❖　❖　❖

So, the prof retiring. Emeritus, he will be. Turning up at the university on his last day of work, in his grey suit, with his battered little case, going to the bursar's office, collecting his superannuation. In cash. He demands it in cash, insists, gets his way. Packing the $30 000 in notes in the case, walking calmly away, never seen again, not by his colleagues, though invited to come back, to lecture, to visit. He never would. He only ever saw one person from the old days, a special student. His heir, I suppose he considered him, the clever young man winning his way to France, and as is hoped for all children, not making his father's mistakes, getting it right, this time.

The usual problem with a good real life story is that it's so often perfect, down to the people's names; you can't bear to change a thing, lest the fluttering of the butterfly wing of chaos send ripples through your fiction that change it utterly. It's a different problem I've got here. Am I going to use my protagonist's names, I mean for instance the one he'd have called that special student by, or stick with my own? I suppose I could use initials; I always find that rather poncy, but it could be useful here. Dr Appleton is my character's name, it's my invention (there's a kind of pointless logic in it), but the thing is, that student didn't appear in the old story, he wasn't one of my characters, though I knew him well, I shared classes with him (there were only two of us) in English, not French, and we graduated at the same time. He was a dancer, quick on his feet; in my memory he glides with graceful haste down linoleumed corridors, through the library and its books, and in seminars his words are as fast as his feet. He's dead now. It's a grim sort of nudge when the friends of your youth die, it topples you out of the sense of your own life for a bit, maybe damages you, a hairline crack or a small chip or even a solid chunk knocked off, and how much more dangerous when it's a mentor outliving his protégé. The father losing the bright hope of his heir.

But this is later, nearly twenty years. We're still back in 1969. Professor Appleton, Professor H, is walking out of the university, out of the town, with his lump sum superannuation payment, $30 000 in notes, in a battered suitcase. Going to Sydney. Beginning his second life's work. The first, the affection of students and their success, the respect and admiration of colleagues, this is thought to have seemed like failure, not at all the luminous career, the great university, the powerful scholarship that he'd hoped, expected; could on the evidence of the impressive monograph on Bandello have achieved. He believed he was a genius, people said. A philosopher who might have changed the course of human thought.

There were also rumours that he wrote crime stories, or thrillers, under a pseudonym, but nobody knew what it was, or had seen any copies of the books.

Professor Appleton, Professor H, offers the form of his life, but not its meanings; offers the events but not his intentions or desires. Offers? The wrong word. They are offered only in the sense that a bribe or a ransom is offered. He'd have kept the exterior as secret as the interior had he been able. Did in fact disguise it in rituals and eccentricity. It was the detective work of anytime acquaintances that compiled the observables, their prurience that made them known. As though the subject's desire for secrecy egged them on. So that the obituary could talk about the canon. The received gossip.

Report follows him to Sydney, and a flat in Ocean Street Edgecliff. He likes the seaside. I had him living in a seedy hotel in the unfashionable end of town, up near the beach, not too far from the power station and the goods yards; this was before the area was tarted up. In his last years in Newcastle he had a room near my mother's house; from our back garden, which was higher than the yard next door and the street, you could see him going in and out of the modest bungalow where he boarded with Mrs Carlsen, a widow. It was only a minute or two from the sea, though I don't know that he ever went there; maybe it was the salt air that he liked. I saw him quite often, but I doubt that he saw me, since I'd have been made invisible by pregnancy and small children, and knew better than to try and catch his eye (you never could, it was irretrievably downcast) or speak across the mental and social and physical spaces that separated us. My mother couldn't imagine why a man like him would live in so mean a place. He has already sold his parents' house; his father was an accountant and K (that's the initial of his odd Christian name) the child of their middle-age, pleasing them one hopes with his doctorate from the University of Paris with highest honours and special commendations of excellence. Such a man, my mother thought, should not be living in working-class gentility at Mrs Carlsen's. He is living up to neither his origins nor his achievements. Nobody gives him credit for achieving a life of the mind, where physical surroundings were not relevant.

◆　◆　◆

His new career is making money. He plays the stockmarket.

His ambition is to make a million dollars; this is the dream he confesses to his investment adviser. So the man says, and presumably truly. It must be the only time in his life that K reveals his heart and mind to another. He will make a million dollars and leave it to his old university to fund a travelling scholarship.

Of course, nobody else knows this. Nobody knows where he is, not even his old fishing partner, drinking gambling swearing Charlie Goffet. (I'm the poet, you're the peasant, K would say to this one-time fellow French teacher.) Charlie, though he often tries to find him by hunting through telephone directories and electoral rolls, can discover no news of him, until his death. Only one person succeeds in keeping in touch, the special student, now a professor himself. If G writes to him—well ahead of time, otherwise K replies with regrets on the grounds that he has been given insufficient notice—then they can meet. Under the clock at Central Station, at 11 am, when they walk to a Greek cafe in Sussex Street, and talk French literature, Pascal, Voltaire, Rousseau, nothing new, K had no time for anything later than 1870. (Though in our classes he recommended modern novels, two a day for the student of French, taken quite fast, not bothering to look up words; the effect would accumulate. This was not for their literary value but for the current language.) The two polite scholars-and-gentlemen in the cafe drinking coffee and talking of literature: this is another story. There is something essentially artistic about it; this is the way men of letters should behave, and *voilà*, so they do. In a strict and rationed manner, and only for two hours; the time up, with charming apology he leaves to walk back to his solitary life. Six months later, if G writes in time, it will happen again.

He was a good lecturer, an excellent speaker on correctly

created public occasions (not intimate or casual ones; they paralysed him); you think of all that store of eloquent elegant English, never spoken. In his head maybe, unless in his room he talked to himself, but this is not currency; it's the servant burying his talent in the earth and therefore it is taken from him. A talent is a weight among the Jews containing 3000 shekels; a talent of silver according to a certain computation (says Alex Cruden MA in 1737, in his 'Concordance to the Bible'; others make it higher) being worth 342 pounds, 3 shillings and 9 pence. The talent of gold was 5475 pounds. No mean sums. And of course this kind of talent was of immense interest to K in his second career; it was the metaphorical biblical kind that he had stopped taking heed of.

By 1983 he has $390 000. He sells the flat in Ocean Street and moves to Glebe, near to Harold Park. Again I could have met him, walking down Glebe Point Road, that was the street he lived in, in a small room at the top and back of an old house. I read at the Harold Park pub during that time, could have passed him in the street, seen him press himself against the fence, head inclined in a kind of bow, eyes refusing to see. Dressed in plastic shoes from K-mart and a tartan K-mart shirt. Would I have recognised him? Now he would be the invisible one: another old derelict shuffling through the days. You don't look at people like that, feeling they have enough to bear without being stared at. His eyes were infested with sores, says the wife of that faithful student, when K went to visit his only friend in hospital during his last illness, walking there as he did everywhere, to save the bus fare.

She tried to get him to see a doctor, but he wouldn't, the fees were too much. Money wasted. Perhaps all he needed was some antiseptic cream? No. He shrugged off her care and she was hardly in a position to insist, she had her mind full of her own troubles. Besides K always shut himself off from women, even when he was teaching them his courtliness made a gulf they couldn't cross. There is of course that suggestion of his being in love with a girl student, which I mentioned in my first story, but I still don't know whether it was mischief, or a lover's tendency to see lovers everywhere, or acute observation. It certainly never showed in his conversation. *Stretch your lips back as though you were saying eee . . . now purse your mouth for an ooo . . .* and out would come a perfect French u. He'd make hideous faces for hours, but never a word of small talk. He wasn't always kind, either. His courtliness was often cruel. The old prof in *Spider Cup*, who asks the 16-year-old student does she know what Existentialism is and when she replies I think so, smiles and says Oh good, you must tell me some time, that was Dr H. You couldn't tell such a man he must have his eyes seen to, for his own good. Though he was beginning not to be able to read. What else was there to do in that poky room, as long as a bed and barely wider, with its laminex table and chrome chair and naked light bulb, where he lived on oranges brought home in brown paper bags, except read?

He's already given most of his books, precious, valuable, rare books, to the university library. Some were vellum-covered eighteenth century editions. He wrote to his successor: 'A student who reads the article on paper-making in the Encyclopaedia will not understand it unless he is able to handle a sheet of XVIIIth Century paper, to roll it between finger and thumb, observe its ribbed texture and so forth.'

It is interesting that it is still the purpose and not the money that moves him. He is not a miser for the sake of it. He still knows that those books are worth more as books than the money they would have fetched, to a new university.

The other evidence offered here, of a sensuous awareness, does not bear thinking of, under the circumstances.

By 1987 he has his million dollars. The stockmarket is lusty and flourishing and his money grows with it. By October he has $1 382 359. His dream has surpassed itself.

In October the stockmarket crashes. In two days he loses $306 000, and the fall doesn't stop there. The million dollars no longer exists; it shrinks to $916 197. How precise these figures are. Not like the anguish they cause.

His friend G writes to try to help him bear it, but K won't be consoled, and then shortly after the financial disaster this sole friend dies. 'Lost his battle with cancer' the newspaper says, as it always does. A battle makes you think of the sword stick Charlie Goffet made for K in the forties, which he wore in his boarding house room in case of attack from political enemies. It suggests clumsy skirmishes, not that ineluctable eroding of the will that is the final consequence of the diseasing of the body. K was filled with shame that he should have been too obsessed with his money grubbing to take notice of his friend's dying. 'Nevertheless it is all I am fit for, at 78 and in bad health.'

Was it the failure of the million, or this untimely death, of a man thirty years younger, that destroyed K's desire to live? Of course it was both, it was everything. Maybe the pinching of the plastic K-mart shoes suddenly became intolerable. Or the juice of an orange too acid on his stomach. It is possible to be precise about sums of money, but anguish isn't computable. What it is is unbearable.

On the twenty-ninth of February his landlord broke into his room because it was three days since he'd seen the professor, for that was what his colleagues in the boarding house called him, thinking it was a nickname, not believing that a real professor would live in such a place. On the twenty-ninth of February, the rarest date on the calendar. That doesn't mean anything, it's just the telling detail that makes a good tale. Offering this curiosity for the mind to puzzle over, unwilling to accept that it has no meaning. The games that careful parents give their children in order to cultivate their puzzle-solving faculties have much to answer for; they train us to believe in solutions. That every piece must fit, in the end.

The landlord, who was called Tony Galego, found K lying on the floor, on his right side. No suspicious circumstances. Death was 'barbiturate poisoning associated with alcohol ingestion'. A lot of Pentobarbitone washed down with whisky, far too much to be an accident. The death was well-done, it worked. The doses not precise, but sufficient.

On the table are two oranges, Valencia they'd be for this is the season of Valencias, they'd be the cheapest. Only in name do they come from the orange groves of Spain, actually growing in the Riverina, Mildura, Sunraysia. Once K thought of retiring to Spain. In my day it was Italy he'd loved. He'd studied in France, he taught the language, but it was Italy he longed for. It was through their languages that he loved places. The canon has him sitting in senate meetings and reading a Spanish Bible, never saying a word. The Bible would have been for the language, not the content. Maybe he smelt Spain in the dense pungent globes of the Valencias, there in the bitter Glebe boarding house, before he died. One of them is decaying; white and blue fur is growing on its skin. Don't forget it's three days, in February, in a small room, under the roof. Beside the oranges are two sheets of paper. The will. The bequest. A travelling scholarship. In a letter to G's widow he wrote that it would give students yet unborn a chance to be like G in what he called the lesser part of books read, places seen, teaching received. His body is to be cremated and the ashes tipped into the sea, with no rites.

But he didn't burn his notebooks or his manuscripts. There they are, his literary failures, in detail: the plots, mostly science fiction, the stories, marked with the name of the magazine he sent them to. And later marked *rejected*. Only ever one accepted, published in America, and paying fifty dollars. Not a sign anywhere of pseudonymous detective stories.

There's a long novel, which those who've read it say is heavily autobiographical, and dealing with murder, sex, spiritualism and philosophy. Since his life seems to have been singularly free of sex and murder he'd have had to make them up. Maybe the violence is the autobiography of an alter ego. I imagine him, taking his scholarly remote austere life and immersing it in bodily fluids, soiling, embroiling, in blood and semen. Getting them out of books. On the other hand, maybe he did know the name of every prostitute in the Cross.

These are the large themes, but what about the minor? How could he manage, since he kept his life free of all those details that novels need? The daily abradings of people, in love and anger, the consolation of connection, however gritty? What about conversations?

The book is called *Remus Leaping*, which must be to do with that Remus who was suckled by a she-wolf, along with his twin brother Romulus, and killed by him when he defied auguries and jumped over the foundations of the city that Romulus was building. Blackest of all sins is fratricide, as Cain knew. This novel was also rejected. I have a fear that K accepted rejection too instantly; I could have told him you must not take no for an answer, must keep on trying; it's often luck when an editor likes your work and you sometimes have to engineer it. It's not like lucky dips where you have only one go. With editors you can keep on trying until the whole tub is empty, so you've got all those chances of finding the packet containing the yes.

I'm not so sure about the treatise on philosophy, called *Optimism*, a work of fascism and science, a vision of a new world ruled by an absolute prince who'll be chosen by machines scientifically measuring his intelligence and personality. K lived into the age of computers but would have no truck with them. A pity; he could have used his clever classical mathematical linguistic brain devising programmes to suit his purpose. Instead he probably didn't even realise the machine for that purpose was at hand. The fascism came from France and the *Action Française* of the thirties and no wonder he was nervous of the secret police: during the war he wanted Hitler to win. Walking round his boarding house room with Charlie Goffet's home-made sword banging against his legs being a solitary brownshirt in spirit. Come to think of it, there was something Prussian in his courtliness. In his Hindenbergian figure.

He wrote the book for future generations, future civilisations even, and he calculated dates in terms of the half-life of radium so they will be able to understand. *Optimism* got rejected by an American publisher in 1950. Only once? What an innocent he was. 'Salut, Dr Appleton' was knocked back by *Quadrant* before *Southerly* took it and that is very nearly a dream run. Five or six rejections is normal, and then perhaps you win a prize. Or else give up. But never after one try. That is indeed a kind of hubris. Pride saying, I will not seek further rejection. People who suffer his serious shyness are often quiveringly proud.

As I said in my first story, he made amateur psychologists of us all.

That story was about me as much as about him. At the end of it I wrote that I wished I'd returned the toast he drank to me, raising his glass in that formal manner of his, at the dinner of the *Alliance Française* in the Edwardian villa called Beau Vista in another Ocean Street. I think I might have made up his doing that. It was a way of showing what a priggish person I was in those days and that any growing out of it I did owed something to him, and so at the end of the story I raised a glass of Muscadet de Sèvre et Maine, at another dinner, in Paris, on the occasion of the immemorial herring, and drank his health. Fictionally speaking. But in fiction the desire becomes the act, and invented or not it exists. And the inventor no longer remembers the one from the other.

But none of this story have I invented. Except the oranges; did you notice them? They are probable, not certain. Though it is also possible that he postponed the suicide until the last Valencia was eaten. And Spain is true. These stories are K's own; all I've done is ordered them a little, looked for right words to tell them in; that's my writer's role, I'm the finder of right words. And there's a nice small irony in the title that I've invented to package it up in: 'Vale Professor Appleton', a Latin farewell from a one-time student who had she had a little of that language, might not have scored such an embarrassment of the elaborate gilt frames he drew in red ink around *bêtises* in the weekly prose. Might have become good at French and possibly something of a special student herself. But no, probably not, being the wrong sex. Vale Professor Hartley.

But not just yet. I have to add the bits he couldn't know. The *post mortem* details. They are ironies as well, but not small. Two of them.

The first is this. After he died the million came back. It wasn't long before it turned into 1.4 million. Notice that the figures have stopped being precise. Point four is all you need: tens of thousands of dollars aren't worth the detail. Less than two years it took. And even in the safety of a bank or a building society it generates interest at a vast rate which is adding on to the capital even as I pen these words. It's reached two million, I heard recently. If this story gets rejected very many times I can keep on updating the figures.

There's the second irony: it's too much money. The annual interest on 1.4 million is $200 000. Far too much to send a single student overseas (and if there were one offering, which is another matter). Imagine the chosen ones, staying at the George V or the Crillon, dining at La Tour d'Argent, sending back the souvenir postcard with the number of the duck they ate on it: Having a great time. Wish you were here. Trying not to think of K H killing himself in a squalid room in a boarding house in Glebe in order to send them there. Trying even harder not to think of him *living* in such a place, the oranges and K-mart shoes and sore eyes, his only occupation or entertainment or interest the stockmarket and its money games.

No. It's too much money. And while the trustees work out what can be done, maybe publishing *Remus Leaping* or endowing a chair, which they'd have to break the bequest to do and so far it's rock solid, it goes on becoming even more too much money.

◆ ❖ ◆

part three

*T*ales
of
Violence
and
Deceit

Mirror
Man

*H*e is a man who goes OS. He comes back with sentences. England, he says, is finished. Only the Arabs flourish. Paris is full of blacks and befouled by terrorists. The city of light is now the city of black and abject fear. English women are frights, so dowdy and dumpy. French women are grubby and too thin. The overblown opulence of Italian women has become disgusting.

He does not suffer from jet lag. He claims to have bent the circadian rhythms to his will. Perhaps because he spends the flight polishing the phrases with which to dismiss the places he's been.

He sees the world with his own eyes. He never sees things as others see them, never as they are. Wherever he goes he creates mirrors. He walks along the streets of Paris and sees himself in the windows of the shops and always with admiration;

in the Beaubourg the Picassos reflect the line of his cheek, in London the Leonardo cartoons limn his profile; in restaurants the looking glasses offer himself to infinity.

When he comes to visit me he always sits in a certain chair, opposite my mother's mirror. Its frame is carved at intervals with brownish gilded roses, and such flowers bloom again deep within its age-stained glass. It's a generous mirror, your face in it has the beauty of an old precious print. He watches himself, as he sits in the chair offering me his sentences. He is a beautiful man, I like to watch him too, ever since that first time I met him at the races and found him more interesting than the horses. Once I moved the chair so he could not see himself, and then he sat sideways, darting glances at me across his profile, and regarding his face in the panes of the cedar cabinet. Managing not to see the blue and white Spode china inside it, shifting his eyes' focus to the glass that protects it. Yet the Spode is one of the reasons he comes to visit me.

I think I shall never go to Florence again, he says. It's done for. The tourists are destroying it, while the Italians, God forgive them for I shan't, connive in that destruction.

I always serve him tea, scented tea as pale and frail as the shallow-bowled cups we drink it from. He holds the saucer on the flat of his palm and lifts the cup to his nose sniffing the fragrant steam. He tips his head back and closes his eyes with pleasure, but leaves a slit at the bottom through which to observe the reflection of this delicate ecstasy. I always put boudoir biscuits on a plate, which he never eats, but I sometimes do. My job is quite demanding, I can afford to. I like the wicked thrill of the sugar gritting my teeth. He looks at the plate and says, Ah here is the lovely Clarice Cliff. You are lucky to have had a clever mother to leave you beautiful things. For of course the Spode and the cedar cabinet and the painted cups and a number of other things I haven't yet mentioned as well as the mirror all belonged to my mother. I love them but wouldn't have acquired them myself. He sees in them great charm because they are inherited, not bought. I would rather have my mother than her beautiful things, I reply, and feel sad that he needs this obvious statement made. At least they invoke her for you, he says.

You may wonder why I accept visits from a man whom my descriptions so far present as really rather a pain. But you see he makes remarks like that, if rarely. A sentence, but moving. Maybe I am waiting to see if his sentences fail him. And I have a fondness for him, scented, formal, frail like the tea. Not needing logic or explanation. Like the tea a minor pleasure. To be enjoyed according to its conventions.

I never knew my mother, he says. She ran away when I was two.

I don't think I believe this. It's a story he's telling me. Himself the forlorn hero. Always the starring role, in pictures, mirrors, tales.

My mother was good with stories, I say. She told them to me all through my childhood, even after I could read she told me stories.

Watching him watching himself, seeing how his shining grey eyes flash mirror to mirror—would that make an infinity of empty silvered surface?—I remember the story of the Snow Queen and the myriad splinters of the magician's evil mirror that entered heart and eye and shrank goodness and beauty while it magnified the ugly and useless. A little shiver of mirror in heart and retina; that would explain the grey flash of his glance. Though I don't know that his mirror eyes are evil, or wicked, simply that they are selfish, self-regarding, their only reflection themselves.

His travelling is always for business, and he guards its mystery. How did it go, I ask, and receive always the same conversational coin in reply, not polished but worn with handling. Business is doing very nicely, he says, thank you kindly. I think of a rich old uncle of ambiguous health, sorely to be missed, but there's the lovely loot . . . I don't know what the business is, other than the breeding of money which can be converted into possessions: the Toorak house, the Mornington Peninsula holiday home, the Porsche for his wife, the Mercedes he doesn't drive to visit me, preferring taxis and no parking problems. Grateful I am it's none of my business.

We don't see each other very often. There are gaps between our meetings. He rings and says, My dear, may I come and drink tea with you? Once I said, No my lover is here, though it wasn't true, and he was put out. He means me to inform my room like the other objects in it, and to be available for his contemplation.

The room is not my life. There is my work, my friends, my lover. He likes to hear about my work, though I cannot offer it in sentences as he does his world. I prattle. Today we took the kids to Cafe Neon for dinner, I tell him. They had a ball. This afternoon we went to the Jag shop in Prahran. The kids liked my shirt, so we took them shopping, it has seconds and samples, very cheap, I get a lot of my clothes there. I like clothes, and I need a lot, since in that ward we don't wear uniform, the cystic fibrosis kids spend so much time in hospital we try to make it like normal life. They don't wear nighties or pyjamas, and all the nurses dress in civvies. Hard to tell the nurses and the patients apart, sometimes. It's a fun place. Now we're all swanning round in Jag shirts and jeans.

I describe the ward to him, and these slender kids who gallop about not obviously sick at all, except for the drips they pull around like friendly triffids and decorate with strange stuffed creatures—they're in theory too old for toys but these count as mascots, fetishes, jokes. And the Ventolin pumps, and the coughing. They spend their lives on the telephone; we have six that can be plugged in by their beds, they wave their legs in the air and yack on endlessly. As teenagers do.

You have quintessentially feminine gifts, he says. I take exception to this. Cystic kids need lots of love. Their prognosis is not good. I care for them. I comfort them. I hurt them to help them. I offer them the affection of gentle hands. It would be a sorry society that saw these things as solely feminine. Ours is a sorry society, he says.

Yes, I say, but not that bad. The caring professions are flourishing. Soon there will be as many men nursing as women. Men who see the skills required as part of their maleness, as women do of their femaleness. He smiles, a little brown withered smile among the brown roses that bloom deep in my mirror. He turns his head and watches his eyebrows arch. You are full of hope, he says. You believe in love, as women do.

As men do, as people do, I insist, but he shakes his head, I can see the mirror offering *sardonically*.

We drink many cups of tea. The round-bellied teapot sits on a frame of silver twigs over a spirit lamp that warms but does not stew. Its handle is insulated with bands of ivory that keep it cool to the grip. We do not talk about my lover, or his wife, though occasionally he makes sentences about her. She is a beautiful woman, he tells me. She likes to buy clothes. She brings up their children carefully. She cooked rare roast beef and Yorkshire pudding when he last returned from OS. I can form no pictures of her from these words. When he tells me that he brought her a necklace of topazes from India, I have no figure to hang the jewels upon but must leave them shut up in their case, blue velvet I imagine it to be and inside creamy satin. I wonder if he offered it to her with lapidary sentences polished on the plane, or the broken phrases of love. He never brings me anything, and I am glad of this, even if we meet once a week there should be nothing between us but pale tea and the uneaten boudoir biscuits.

He walks about the room, the saucer on the flat of his palm, his fingers which he curls like a mouse in his hand steadying the cup. He pauses in front of the break-fronted bookcase that matches the Spode cabinet, with his head on one side. You have a lot of books, he says. I know he isn't looking at their titles but at the shape of his head in the glass. Faint censure in his tone, as if books are possessions like any other and I have too many, as though they were a hundred or a thousand teacups. I like to read, I say. He doesn't know because he's never seen it that the four walls of my bedroom are covered with bookshelves. There's only room for the bed; you have to get into it from the foot, crawl up to the pillows like a woman of the harem entering the sultan's bed. My lover and I take turns at being the sultan reclining on the pillows while the other creeps up under the doona. The passage can be boisterous or liquid and sensuous or passionate or friendly. My tea friend doesn't know this either; it is not a subject for conversation.

He is still apparently looking at the titles of my books, turning his head slowly, but in reality observing his reflection. The light falls on it from one source, and as he turns his head the planes are lit then darken. He might be a classical sculpture on a plinth, slowly revolving so that its workmanship may be admired.

He moves to the Spode cabinet, and perhaps this time he really is looking at the blue and white Chinese ware inside. This room is a jewel, he says, it's a perfect work of art.

Not at all, I reply, it is I who am the jewel. The room is my setting. It's mine, like my clothes; I wear it when it suits me.

Perhaps I am seeing too much of this man. I might begin to talk in sentences too.

❖ ❖ ❖

The ward recreation officer takes the cystic kids to the Show. They come back loaded with bags and stuffed with sweets. Nobody eats any dinner. You can't blame them; it's canneloni, but dry as old leather. The meals are delicious only in name: chicken cacciatore, sweet and sour pork. One of the girls bought a red plush devil as fat as three five-year-old children; she keeps it on her bed and everybody who comes into the room has an irresistible desire to hide it. Perhaps because it is the most utterly unhidable object imaginable everybody wants to try. She can always find it again, though there is a lot of joking but violent recrimination. The kids are very hard to settle, they need a lot of calming, a lot of soothing, of lap-sitting while the paperwork is done. Some of these kids are pretty much as tall as me, and they like to sit on laps and rest their heads on your shoulder. Their sharp little bum bones stick into you. No flesh to cushion. I'm late finishing the shift—nothing new— don't get home till past eleven. He rings after an absence and asks to come round. I'm showered and wearing a kimono, not ready yet for bed. Whatever the hour I like a gap between work and sleep. My lover is a nurse too, we both work odd shifts, which is one reason why we don't live together.

I lean over the narrow balcony and smoke a cigarette. I can hear the melancholy roar of the traffic in Gatehouse Street, the grating of brakes as the trucks clash to a stop at the lights; in the garden next door a tree groans softly in the night-wind. When his taxi turns the corner I duck under the tall sash window that seems intended to discourage balcony use and pull the curtains across it.

He's been to Houston and Denver and New York on this trip. I'm saving up to go overseas but it won't be as he does. I'll live in places and learn them, a nurse can always get work and I'm highly qualified. Including a diploma in Intensive Care with special reference to children; I love that work but can only stand it for six months or so at a time, it's too intense. I'm a bit envious of his capacities to travel but he makes so little of them, seems to travel in order to belittle, that my envy doesn't take hold. I look in the brown flowered mirror to tidy my shower-damp hair and offer it a sardonic smile in anticipation of the attention he will pay it when he comes.

He's wearing a jumper and is agitated. He shakes my hand as always when we meet but not politely, hanging on to it, not letting go. He babbles. His sentences have broken. David, my dear, he says. Where to . . . I don't . . . what can I . . . it doesn't . . . little sharp shards of sense that I cannot assemble into meaning. Tea, I say, and he shakes his head. Would you, he says, do you mind . . . could I ask . . . He casts his eyes around the room. He's not looking for or at himself. Whisky, I offer, and he nods, and when he's drunk it he begins to tell me what has happened, halting, repetitive, stumbling, but this time I piece his meaning together. He has come back from overseas to find that he has lost his wife. She's left him, or rather, she's asked him to leave, she wishes to stay in the house with the children, it's hers, she can, it's in her name for the tax, she has the right, well financially though morally may be a different matter, her lover has moved in with her there's no longer any place for him there. I see a woman hand on hip, the other pointing, blonde hair flaring, saying Go! Around her neck topazes.

David, he says, could I . . . would you mind . . . do you

think I could . . . would it be a nuisance . . . with you . . . for a bit . . .

I put more whisky in his glass. I tell him no. Gently, being very sorry. I tell him that my lover now lives with me. It's a lie, but he believes it. I show him the tiny bookcase bedroom. He can see that there's no place for him in this apartment. The drawing-room with the cedar and the Spode, the oval dining-table, the japanned tin trunk where the teapot sits on its silver twigs, it's full, there's not even a sofa to doss on.

The tears of love melted the splinters of the evil magician's mirror, but I have only a fondness to offer, a scented formal frail fondness not passionate or fiery enough to melt ice. A delicate scented breath not strong enough to mist let alone melt.

I shall have to go to an hotel, shan't I, he says.

Come and have a cup of tea tomorrow, I say. He looks at me with his silvered eyes. Thank you. The picture of him sitting on the chair opposite the mirror, teacup in hand, sniffing the steam is there for a moment as I offer, he accepts, and then it fades, becomes a shadow, is invisible, might never have been. The mirror frames the cabinet, the Spode blue in its dim depths, the edge of a painting; nobody is there.

I close the door behind him and think of the story of the swineherd-prince who made a saucepan with bells on it that played a song:

Ah, dear Augustine,
All is lost, lost, lost

Nonsense, I tell myself. Why lost? This could be the saving of him. Pain and fear and anguish doing their own mirror melting, so he can see the world as it is, as it sees itself, and not just with his own eyes.

The bells go on tinkling the words in my head. *Lost . . . lost . . . lost.* Once I start thinking of a song I can't stop.

❖   ❖   ❖

Next evening the ward is its usual chaotic self. Melanie's monstrous red plush devil is hidden again, she accuses everybody of stealing it. There's a fight going on over the last of the Show Mars Bars. Someone is singing at the top of his voice and being pummelled for it. The television set bangs away unregarded. Its noisy eye is lit from early morning till late at night though rarely is it attended to. Except for 'Neighbours'. But people can't bear not to have it on. It seems to be a kind of comfort, keeping the noisy echoing silence of the hospital at bay; they're saved from its seriousness by this racket from the outside world. Suddenly the room empties; a race for the gold phone down the corridor, Melanie pursuing her devil next door, others to the kitchen to make toasted sandwiches; all evening there'll be these eddies of noise and movement to and fro. I stay to pull the curtains, order the beds for the eventual night's sleeping. The television catches my attention, it's the evening news. Suburban horror. Again? Toorak killings. There's a picture of a half-timbered Tudor house, nothing fake about its prosperity. I stand and watch, picking dead daffodils out of a vase of spring flowers. Shrouded stretchers carried out. A photograph superimposed of a blonde woman, smiling. I wonder if she would wear topazes. The newsreader offers urgent words, in clusters, without connections. (Lead us not into causation.) Society woman . . . lover . . . mystery double shooting . . . murder . . . murder–suicide . . . suicide pact . . . The beds are full of crumbs. I brush them out by feel, keeping my eyes on the set. The Toorak house again. The mirror man lives in Toorak. The newsreader is enjoying the Toorak house; the disasters of the rich and fortunate have a particular pizazz. So much more momentum. So much further to fall into misery. Such a satisfying thump. The newsreader gets on to the husband, of course there's a husband ... Calm as plastic she offers him ... bereaved ... or a killer ... mourning, rejoicing ... the television is too clever to say. It leaves you to piece the possibilities together for yourself. I don't believe the mirror man, dismissive eloquent contemplator of himself among the teacups, is implicated. I think of his grey eyes no longer self-reflecting, of him too miserable to polish phrases; perhaps he can't bear what he sees; can't bear seeing the world as it is. Even my fondness failing him.

The room erupts in kids again. Melanie has got the devil back, but it is only a matter of time and noise before it's carried away again. The television is discussing whether it'll be Hawthorn or Carlton on Saturday. Now the kids are quiet and watch breath-bated waiting for the desired definitive word. In this room Hawthorn.

I hope the mirror man is safe.

I

Love

You

*Y*es, that's her. She's gorgeous, isn't she. Those long legs. I love a woman with long legs. Like a young horse. They have nervous legs, delicate, full of energy. You can tell, she's just arrived, come galloping up the hill and skittered to a stop when she saw the writing on the car. We'd had a pretty grotty trip, dust and rain and mud. There was a good thick coating to make the marks in.

True? Of course. Yes, I did love her. She knew that. Came up the hill, saw the writing, turned round, and I took the shot just as she stood, poised, with that sexy pleased look. She was photogenic, you didn't need to pose her, any fleeting moment you caught her she looked good.

Of course shooting her wasn't the object of the outing. Shooting anything, really, though I had my camera along and got some nice photographs of the lake. There was a kind of silver light that day, and I thought, this is peace, and I photographed it, I thought I am actually photographing peace. There was nobody around, no human noises. It's hard to get away from human noises. There's always our machinery cutting the silence into shreds. Lawn mowers or cars or chain saws, even those screaming little things for beating up cakes. She didn't talk much, and anyway she had a soft voice, husky and slow, she'd always talk in a murmur, and there was the water making a liquid lapping sound against the pebbles, and no wind to rustle the leaves. No sun, either. Have you noticed how noisy the sun makes things when it shines? The bright light and the bright noise. I liked the greyness and calmness.

We walked around the shore for quite a bit. She didn't have any shoes on, she liked to travel light, that bird. It was rocky, but she picked her way, the rockiness didn't bother her. There were little sandy coves and thick mats of reeds washed up and sometimes shingle; she said she liked the feel of all the different surfaces of the earth under her feet. In among the rocks there were these small patches of grass, the kind that grows around lakes, thick and lush with little soft blades that don't prickle at all when you lie on them, even with no clothes on.

Yeah, we made love. I'm not always . . . I mean, I can sometimes. I suppose it was the peacefulness, all that quiet emptiness, the silvery grey lake and the sky and the water lapping. It worked in the straight way, normal, her on her back and those legs around me and it was slow and sort of kind and afterwards we just lay on the grass and yes I did love her and she loved me. She had a tattoo on her bottom, on the left side, a dragonfly she said it was. I thought its wings shimmered when she moved. You know, she'd twitch her bum and the different colours of its wings'd shimmer. I thought it just suited her, a dragonfly, because of them being long and slender and big-eyed. I haven't got wings, she said, and I said where's your imagination girl. I see wings.

It was cool there, not cold, we didn't feel cold, but the air was cool and sort of dry. There was this faint watery breeze off the lake, but it wasn't humid, not that jungle humid where your skin can't breathe. When you're sweating and the atmosphere's sweating and there's nowhere for it to go. And for a bit I thought, I could stay here forever, but of course you never can. Not in the good places. We put our clothes on and walked back around the shoreline. There weren't even any boats pulled up. I wished I had one of those old wooden boats that people used to go fishing in, I could see myself carrying down the oars and setting off in the dawn, that's what it felt like, without the sun, the light all clear and grey like that, it felt like a dawn, the day not begun yet. And you push the boat out, you're wearing old sneakers in case of oyster shells or sharp rocks on the bottom, and you crawl in, and the oars make a quiet splash as they pull you through the water. You know the right places for the fish, and drop the anchor over, and bait your hooks with pongy old bits of green prawn, and throw the lines in, and you sit and wait for the fish to bite.

Of course it was the afternoon then, and too late in the day for fishing, even if we'd had a boat, with oars in it, and lines, and bait. We walked back to where we started, where the hill came down from the road. We didn't walk up the slope together. I felt good, I didn't need her right beside me at that moment. She'd stopped to look at something growing, the hillside had little scrubby plants with flowers on, she liked to look at things like that. Not pick, as I said she travelled light, she just looked. Well, when I say she travelled light, I don't know about in her head. Who knows what's in people's heads. And maybe she didn't carry much baggage with her because of what she took along in her head. Stuff you'd like to chuck away, but you can't. If you could pack it all up in a port and leave it behind in a motel, with a false name and lost property never catching up with you. Lost property: I should be so lucky.

So I walked up the hill on my own, her mooning over some plant, and the choppers went over. You can't even see their blades whirling, just the air disturbed. The choppers went over and they chopped the sky in pieces and it fell down in chunks around me and I raced up the hill but still there was this noisy sky falling in chunks all round me. I couldn't get away. I got in the car but it didn't help. I got out and waited for her and that was when I wrote the words in the dirt on the side of the car. The choppers were gone by then but the quiet was still falling in pieces around us. Sharp pieces, heavy, that do damage.

She wasn't hurrying, it was the plants she cared about, bending and touching them as though it would make them feel better, but finally she stopped that and came galloping up the last bit of hill to the top and saw the words and skittered round and leaned and stood the way you see her there, poised on her toes lifting her head back offering her throat with that slow pleased smile and pulling her shirt down in her rather shy way with her big kind knuckly hands so careful of the flowers and that was when I shot her, first with the camera and then with the gun and then the camera again. You can see what the camera is about to pick up, just there in the corners of her mouth, the doubt that will turn into amazement, here, in this one, when she sees I've got the gun, the amazement already sliding into fear as she realises what I'm going to do, here, and when I've done it, when I've pulled the trigger, haven't I, there's the writing on the car smudged where she fell across it.

It's a good camera, you see you only need one hand. I wanted a good camera, I wanted to take good pictures, you have to try to do things well. These pictures turned out well, even using only one hand. The gun behaved well too. The noise of the gun isn't like the noise of the choppers, it doesn't chop the sky into pieces falling on your head, it's an orderly sound, that puts things back. The noise of the gun rings like a bell and all the sky is back in place again and everything is very very quiet.

The writing? I used the gun. I guess it scratched the duco. It didn't seem to matter at the time.

Tale
Telling

A friend of mine told me this story. We were sitting in the back room of a restaurant, which was the bar and snacks, drinking white wine, catching up with one another. Cass had asked me how my novel was going, and I'd said, well, I was writing a lot, but I was worried that nothing ever happened. People had social gatherings, and talked and thought, but that was about all. Still, I was planning on putting in a suicide, that should make for a bit of action, it was at least a violent event. But then, perhaps it would seem contrived. When I get started I can talk for hours about my novel. But I don't want advice. Just reassurance.

Well, she says, suicides do happen. In fact a lot of people commit suicide, or try to. Her face twists. She's just heard about an old friend, she's still feeling upset.

I say it isn't a major character that will do it. It's one of the lesser ones, sort of pointing up the options open to the heroine (if you can call her that); she could do this, but doesn't, she chooses survival, there but for the grace, and all that.

Cass wants to tell me about her suicide. Talk, not listen. He was a young man, when she knew him, an electrician, who came to their house to mend the telly. She was just a kid at the time, fifteen or so, he probably ten years older. He was terrifically good looking, blond hair, golden skin, handsome shoulders, but more than that, he was nice, he talked to her. He didn't have to, she was just a kid, but he made her feel he liked chatting her up. His eyes shone, his face crinkled, he smiled. I got the impression the telly took a lot of fixing.

Naturally, Cass got a crush on him. She would've even if he hadn't noticed her. There were two buses she could catch to school, one from the corner a block away from her house, or she could walk two miles to the village (this was in England) and catch a bus there. In the village was the electrical shop he and his brother kept. So every day she walked that two miles, just to go past the shop, just so she might walk past that shop and just might see him, there, inside, blond and handsome, serving the customers.

Was he married?

Oh no; not then. Not till much later. His brother was, though. This married brother flirted with her a bit too, it was a sort of game, well, it probably was for the other one as well. Once, it was funny, she'd been standing at the bus-stop and the brother had been driving past in his van and waved at her, hanging out the window, waving, grinning; he'd driven into the bus. Not concentrating on his driving, see. Nobody hurt, but the van a bit wrecked. His wife never spoke to her again. But the younger one, the one she found so thrilling, who always talked to her, he was a bachelor.

Cass's eyebrows lift, her eyes widen, her face smooths; she's a fifteen-year-old girl whom men like to chat up at the bus-stop. Who has men do foolish things by just looking at her.

The young one, the bachelor, he kept it going, beyond that. Took her on a picnic, they sat under willows by a river, a flat still sort of river with grassy banks, it's still in her mind's eye. The unlined candid eye of the girl, seeing again that river of her former home, so different from the rocky broken rivers here. He held her hand and kissed her. That was all. It was just what she wanted. Romance. Well, at fifteen one does. But wasn't it thoughtful of him, knowing that was just right for her, when he was so much older, and had slept with plenty of women?

Maybe that was how he knew.

Probably. Anyway, she'd often thought gratefully of him because of that.

Then what happened?

Well, nothing. She got older, went away to university, got married, migrated. And he, twenty years later, committed suicide. Last year, that was.

But why? How?

Drank a bottle of whisky, took a bottle of pills. Drove up to a local beauty spot, sat in the car. That gets to her, somehow, his going there. Sitting in the car at a famous beauty spot, choosing as his last view of the world the peaceful smooth downs, and in the distance, a chalk horse—do I know those strange monumental horses, larger than life, ancient, drawn on the downs? She sees him looking at that, drinking the whisky, swallowing the pills.

It's sympathetic. The ancient landscape—no, its unnerving. To kill himself there meant that the landscape failed. Perhaps he sat in the car, whisky and pills ready but not finally accepted, waiting for that beloved countryside to save him. And it didn't.

So he had to take them. But the easy death, more or less easy, that is something to be grateful for. Neither of us likes to think of violent means to the already violent act, the wrist-cutting, brains-blowing, the jumping from high buildings, or railway bridges in the path of trains, the insistence on blood and mess to make the survivors suffer.

Yes, that's the way I'd choose, if I were to think of it which I don't, I add hastily, let's not tempt fate by admitting the possibility. Life has not been that bad yet. The cowardly way people would call it, says Cass, but why not choose a comfortable end when there's an option.

A waitress comes to take our order, cold tongue or chicken pie, bread, salad. We order another bottle of wine, the house white, we sip a lot in the pauses of the narrative. This back room is a pleasant enough place, except perhaps for the large numbers of men in natty suits who stand about the bar, one hand in pocket, the other round a glass, their legs slightly apart and very straight between the knife-edged creases of their trousers; frequently they throw their heads back and laugh loud ritual laughs full of teeth. What are they? Public servants, lawyers? Not journalists. Perhaps party men, or lobbyists. Cass hopes they don't have people's destinies in their hands; they probably do.

And this young man, the electrician, *why* did he do it?

Ah. Dreadful things had happened. The brother, the one who ran into the bus, he came home one night very late, very drunk, and murdered his wife. Strangled her with the electric jug cord. Sort of tool of his trade, you might call it.

My God. But *why*? Was it a crime of passion? As they say.

In a way, but in reverse. He had a mistress, he was seeing her, was presumably sick of his wife. Wanted to be rid, to divorce, and chose not law but violence.

Neither of us can cope with this. Had the wife been having an affair and the husband killed her in a mad fury of betrayal, of jealousy, it might have been more bearable, it might have been tragic, like Othello. Even if he got it wrong. A kind of poetic justice, however bleak still logical. Instead the poor wife had been betrayed twice over. Of course, Cass says, he was very drunk at the time. Came home, strangled her, fell into a drunken stupor, woke up in the morning and saw what he'd done. Well, his eight-year-old daughter came and woke him and showed him. He rang the police, said somebody's murdered my wife, but there was never any doubt he'd done it, no sign of break-in or robbery, he the only one there. He was tried, convicted, put in gaol. He might be out now, it was eight years ago.

The food comes, the waitress brings plates and salad, bread sprinkled with chives, the second bottle of wine. We're sitting in comfortable canvas chairs, under a skylight hung with massive ferns. The waitress brings cutlery wrapped in paper napkins, we sit with the watchful expectant air of people about to be fed. Our eyes glance about. The walls are hung with curious paintings of haloed naked saints, or Christs perhaps, in the company of women naked too, perhaps they are holy whores, or their wives. In some they're taking saunas. The painting are for sale. We've agreed they don't appeal to us. Chemical sweets in lolly wrappings.

We're eating hungrily enough. Cass's tale hasn't put us off our food. But it isn't finished yet.

And the other brother, her electrician, was he married by then?

Oh yes, says Cass, and that's another thing. She sighs, the memory of that golden infatuation of her youth, of the kind beautiful young man so come to grief, oppresses her. Even though it happened far away in time and space, and she's only just learned the details, from her mother visiting, venturing away from that small village life where nothing is secret. The mother smugly, nervously, eyeing Cass; a dreadful thing for the parents, such nice ordinary people, you never know. Such a thing will never happen in her family, will it.

Oh yes, Cass says, there's more to come. His wife committed suicide, the year before him. Went to town and up the highest building she could find, it was a small town and the buildings weren't terribly high but high enough, and jumped off. Died almost instantly. All this business of the brother, the murdered sister-in-law, was thought to have preyed on her mind, she couldn't live with it. She'd become more and more depressive, an ordinary clinical condition presumably, and so had he, the two of them weighed down by this family crime, not able to go on bearing it. And their children, they left two children, small, just going to school; think how terribly life must have become too much for them, to be able to leave their children like that, one after the other.

I notice the artifice in Cass's apparently random and certainly unrehearsed telling of this story, her ordering of events for maximum pity and terror. It's only at this point that she piles on the bit about the other wife's suicide. The narrative can hardly hold together under the weight of it. No wonder it was all too much for the young electrician, in his forties now, to bear. It makes you feel unsteady, yourself; these young chaps prospering, business good, wives, children, everything going for them, and all gone to nothing. Four hundred years ago the teller of such a tale would have discoursed upon the theme of Mutability, all is Mutability, on this cold earth beneath the moon. Nothing has changed.

The wife, adds Cass, jumping from that high-enough

building, didn't actually land on the ground. She fell on to a mini, belonging to a girl who'd just bought it, saving her money to buy the little red car she'd always wanted. Made a mess of it, in fact. The girl tried to get compensation, since it wasn't insured, but nobody would have it on, it was nobody's responsibility. She wrote letters to the paper, and everybody agreed it was a terrible shame, but there was nothing to be done.

We're drinking coffee now, looking at the pictures of the laid-back saints, or Christs, or maybe they're just old-fashioned beatified hippies. Cass says, so you see, suicide's pretty common. Even among ordinary people. So's murder for that matter. Commonplace, when you look at the papers.

Of course she's right. I see the form, the shape, the superlative repetitive horror of the pattern life has made. But I can't see how I can possibly use it. Not in a work of fiction. Not that sort of truth. Life may be like that, but art isn't.

I go back to inventing my suicide. Of a minor character, in a single chapter, cleanly, with sadness, not much horror. Drown her, swiftly, kindly, in an icy lake, the whole deed only seconds long. My heroine contemplates it and is safe.

The Power
of Words

I suppose if some inspiration,
or catalyst, or even just a beginning, were to be identified, it
would be that enthusiastic teacher getting us to read *'Tis Pity
She's a Whore*, devising a very serious course of Elizabethan
and Jacobean tragedy because she was so proud of us, an
exceptionally and quite amazingly clever group of girls in an
already academic private school. Anglican, it was, but more in
name than deed, and we the daughters of the affluent: *nouveau
riche* or established middle class, or even faintly aristocratic,
like my father, who is a diplomat, here on a posting from our
native land, which we've almost never lived in.

I'm particularly good at English, as is doubtless apparent from
my vocabulary and my control of syntax, and of course
punctuation, though I suspect I am overly fond of the semi-colon.
But I can learn to control that. I am going to be a writer, indeed

I am, witness the setting down this; one must remember all experience, and find the words for it; until then it doesn't exist.

I imply that our teacher and her delight in mind expanding was to blame, but that's not really true. It would have happened anyway. But nevertheless I think of that night, sitting with Simon in the library, doing our homework, me reading *'Tis Pity She's a Whore*, as the beginning.

But first, the play. Nobody much reads it any more—in fact George Steiner says that one of the great problems of literature these days is that nobody is well-read any more, you can't assume acquaintance with Dante or Milton or even the Bible. So all those great windows opening on the endless vistas of other people's minds and giving an extra dimension to quite ordinary writings, are thickly curtained with ignorance. Each book is its own little dark cell, claustrophobic. Thus is appreciation cabbin'd, cribb'd, confin'd. Shakespeare, you see; but even he is little more than a series of peepholes these days. Of course I am not going to let this ignorance happen to me; already I read voraciously, and always real literature. Certainly, *'Tis Pity* isn't a really great play, not a patch on Shakespeare's, or things like *The Duchess of Malfi*, but if you don't compare it with such towering works of art, then it's really very good. It's about a sister and a brother who are in love with one another; everybody else around seems boring and ugly in comparison. But alas the girl gets pregnant and has to marry one of her suitors, who discovers her condition, hardly surprising, and swears revenge. But pretends friendliness, and invites everybody to a party, intending to unmask the lovers. The brother goes, although he knows what is planned, but first kills his sister and turns up with her heart on his dagger. Of course he's killed, though he has his revenge on the husband first, and there's quite some carnage to end the play. It's really powerful stuff.

So there I was, in the library, thoroughly enjoying the blood and violence and dramatic speeches, unable to keep quiet about it, so that finally Simon's attention was drawn. We always sat diagonally opposite one another at the long refectory table, which ran across one side of the room. On the other was a sofa, in front of the fireplace, but we mostly worked at the table, with all the dictionaries and reference books to hand. It was— indeed it is: I find I have trouble with tense here, wanting to write in the past because that is where events belong, and yet the house still is, the table still there and the sofa, quite unchanged—so, it was and is a very fine room, and our favourite in the house, partly because we felt that it was the one most thoroughly ours. Our parents hardly ever went there; they were out a lot, endless dinners, receptions, functions of one sort or another. Daddy had a study off the bedroom; he and Mummy spent a lot of time up there. Or else entertaining, in which case unless it was a really big party the library was a good quiet place to be. The house was quite nice, though not the best we've had: rather dull architecturally but very large and comfortable. Of course it belongs to our government. It had— the past tense still insists—a pool in the back garden, which we'd made use of all summer and for the first time in ages we were sun-tanned. I remember looking at Simon's arm lying across the table, and the delicate golden brown colour of it, and the way the fine fuzz of hair was aureoled by the lamplight.

Simon and I are twins—still, still—and very beautiful; that's simply a fact. We see it when we look at each other. Of course it's emphasised for others by there being two of us. People are always being amazed by us, so beautiful and so alike. I've heard it said that twins never really separate, that their early closeness remains with them always, at least so often as they live together, and often even apart. Simon and I never quarrelled, and always liked the company of one another better than anybody else. All the more so because we'd moved around so much, every few years in a different country, and it was easier to be friends with one another than always be about the wearisome business of forming new relationships. Of course we're not identical twins, since we are definitely of opposite sexes, oh quite definitely; we are not halves of one egg, but from the moment of conception we have been together, and our bodies and our minds are very alike.

We're both slender, fair, the sort of structure that is considered aristocratic, with fine bones and delicate features, nothing coarse or peasanty. Grey eyes and fair hair, silvery fair, not yellow, not at all gaudy, and it pleases us to wear it in the same style, short and in curls all over our heads. And that summer, with our suntans, we took to wearing white, because it was so plain and simple and dramatic against the brown.

Although I was a beauty I was not much followed by boys. This didn't worry me at all, since I met very few, and they were quite immature. I knew that when I went out into the world and met real men they would know what I was worth. Of course the girls at school raved over their immature boys and were always getting violently involved with this or that one, but it all seemed so very crude to me. Crass. In the Christmas holidays Mummy suggested we have a pool party for our schoolmates but Simon and I talked it over and decided it would be so noisy, such a bore, all those kids hanging about. Simon has the same view of the locals as I. So we swam, and lay in the sun reading, and were quite content with ourselves. Simon enjoys serious reading as much as I, though he has to concentrate on languages, since it is intended that he follow Daddy's profession.

That night he looked up from the French translation he

was doing (we were both in our second last year of school and it was important to do well) and pretended to sigh.

'Well, come on Nell,' (he always calls me that, but no one else can, my real name is Elinor), 'don't keep it to yourself any longer. What's so fascinating?'

'It's a seventeenth-century play, on a very trendy subject.'

'What, love and death, I suppose. All those old plays are.'

'Yes, but with a difference . . .'

'Well?'

'Incest.'

'Ah,' said Simon, 'very trendy.'

'Not the kind the papers are full of, the ugly violent raping kind, with people forced against their will, but a beautiful loving kind, the couple in love, in fact, all quite mutual.'

'What are they?'

'Oh, brother and sister, of course.'

'Ah,' he said again, his grey eyes shining across the table at me, 'I must read it.' So I stretched out my hand across the table to pass him the book, and saw my arm, haloed with delicate hairs against the brown, reaching out, meeting his, his arm so like mine and yet not mine, his.

He read the play too. It was autumn, the weather was chilling. We covered up our lovely golden flesh against the cold. Sometimes Simon would light a fire in the library fireplace, and we would sit on the sofa and read, and make toast when the logs were red and glowing, and drink tea. I loved the fire, it made the room so much a world of its own, a world absolutely ours, full of mysterious life like the flames that leaped in the chimney piece. By the time the winter came we'd both read the play several times (I wrote a brilliant essay on it and got a very high mark for it) and talked it over endlessly. Talked about ourselves endlessly. And did not confine ourselves to talking. Perhaps it was my hand that first stroked the springing virile hairs of his arms, perhaps his fingers that first explored the intricate curves of my ear half hidden under silvery curls identical with his; neither of us had the sense of being first. As always, we moved together.

Our story, this record that I am writing now, has hadly an unexpected climax. A sensitive reader has surely seen where it is tending. I am not writing it as a work of fiction, to catch unawares with the surprise of its outcome. Fiction will come later, when I have dealt with my life, our lives. But I want the reader to understand as well as perceive, to see the inevitability as we did. We didn't become lovers without knowing what we were doing, without discussing it first, without feeling we could do nothing else. We had always loved one another absolutely, and now we were in love with our almost mirror images. We touched and wondered and probed the depth of our own grey eyes. We lay before the fire and made love with our delicate beautiful bodies, caressing our whitening skins voluptuous on the oriental rug. It pleased us to see our bodies so alike and yet with such amazing differences lying together.

We were very careful of course not to be caught. When our parents went out we would fall to, and by the time they came home would be quietly at the table working, or drinking tea on the sofa, or chastely asleep in our own beds. But the excitement of our relationship filled our lives. There was the passion and the sensuality of our physical connection—seventeen is a great age for sex, though Simon teased me with being an old lady compared to Juliet who was barely fourteen, and he just right for Romeo—and as well another kind of dark and creepy excitement. The pleasure that comes when you do something you know is wrong (our morals were as cultivated as our manners) not because it is wrong but because that dark and shameful excitement that the act gives you makes you realise why it is forbidden. You think of pacts with the devil and selling your soul, and then you think of the soul residing where the heart is and you feel it already constrained, already nervous as if it knew you had contracted it away. It's an intermittently aching tooth, that you can't resist trying for the *frisson* even of pain that it gives. We are gluttons for experience to seek the dreaded so greedily.

But it was a kind of luxury, that guilt. The luxury of lechery, and incestuous at that. A gilding with guilt. We enjoyed it, but did not entirely believe in it. It was the least important part of our relationship; the real part was the congress of our bodies and minds, and the real fear was that someday we might be separated. We both knew that we could not think of anyone else as lover. The slightest glance at the idea filled us with disgust. But we were mostly confident that we need never be parted.

We weren't superstitious either about comparing ourselves with the unluckily incestuous Giovanni and Arabella, or Romeo and Juliet the star-crossed lovers. Fate after all has to work with the manners and problems of the time, and we had circumvented or solved such as were their downfall. I'm not much of a believer in progress—after all who has bettered Shakespeare—but in some things the world has improved. Arabella's dreadful end came from getting pregnant; I profiting from that warning had been to the Family Planning Clinic of infinite discretion and got the pill. Both unfortunate heroines fell foul of that bad old parental habit of marrying daughters to the most attractive bidder, which would not at all be my problem. My parents had no intention of marrying me off to anybody, and would be most put out if I married myself before my university education was finished, and for a while after that. Meanwhile, Simon and I could live perfectly well, under our parents' roof, and must only take care that when we left it we could be together. Through university, and even through Simon's diplomatic career. Spinster sisters keeping house for bachelor brothers is an archaic custom that could well be revived. And I could go on with my writing and reading, both richly fed by my private and public life. All in all, our romantic and rosy future seemed as feasible as our passionate present.

Yet we were caught, and not by carelessness or anything that we could have avoided. Fate, or accident; call it what you will, it put an end to us. Our parents came home unexpected and caught us. They'd had a collision with another car on their way out to dinner, minor but frightening, and by the time the police business had been gone through wanted only to come home. They returned in a taxi which we might have heard but which did not impress itself upon our ears as would have the Mercedes crunching up the drive. They walked into the library—they knocked but didn't wait—and found us naked on the sofa.

Simon was sent to boarding school in England, and after all the harsh words—the vocabulary was sometimes different from the finale of *'Tis Pity She's a Whore* but the meanings were the same—and the anger, came my mother's sorrow.

'Elinor, tell me please, I want to understand. *Why* did you do it?'

'Because we love one another, and people who love one another make love with one another.'

I could see that was not an answer that helped. She tried another question.

'Didn't you know it was wrong?'

Wrong. I remembered the dark shameful excitement. The pleasure of guilt that was finally irrelevant. We'd known it was wrong, but it was also so right for us that the right prevailed, absolutely. But I did not say that.

181

They sent me to a convent in Melbourne to finish my education. A convent, in the second last decade of the twentieth century; in the midst of modernity we are medieval, and I suppose the fact should please me. They didn't want to have me near them any more. Not being able to believe in fact that I am their child. Of course they mean metaphorically. But why not literally? Call me changeling, devil's spawn. Suppose my mother coupled with an incubus disguised as my father, and the beautiful twins the offspring of that demon possession.

Not that I believe that. My sense of our innate and perfect virtue is so strong, the guilt is simply decoration, the idea of evil simply a flirtation with words—a temptation I can never resist. But incest is no different from eating pork, forbidden only for the health of primitive societies. An anthropological anachronism. We should have been princes in Egypt.

Instead, a convent, and a boarding school. A dull end, you might say. Not like Juliet's, or Arabella's. No daggers, self-inflicted or wielded by a raging brother. Simon did not rip me open and turn up at one of the parents' parties with my heart on the end of his weapon. But then I wasn't pregnant, nor did I have a husband seeking revenge. We live according to the mores of our time. So, though our story began with *'Tis Pity* it doesn't end with it. It hasn't ended yet. I am a writer and I write in a happy ending. Future joy from present suffering. I cannot write to Simon, but I can write down that. One day our two halves will be made whole and life will have meaning again.

So there it is, in words, it exists, nothing can undo it.

Tryst

—*D*id you get it, he said, as soon as he'd drawn her inside the little house and shut the fragile front door.

She opened her schoolbag and took out an object wrapped in an old silk scarf.

He didn't unwrap it, but held it in his hands slowly feeling its shape.

Why does your mother have such a thing?

—Ever since we had burglars once. She says it makes her feel safer.

—Has she ever used it?

—No. My father says she'd have to be so close she'd never dare.

They talked coldly, not really interested in the words; the questions and their answers a ritual, what was due to the opening of the package, which fixed the eyes and even more the minds of both. He felt the shape through the wrapping still; it was very hard, very solid. He began to fold back the silk.

—I suppose it's really rather pretty, he said, regarding the handle, black enamelled with bands of ivory, the silver chasings so elaborate the eye could lose itself in them, wondering at the art lavished on an object meant for doing, not contemplating. The strained wooden house about them was witness to the tenuousness of staying alive; the useless beauty of this small lethal object was foreign in it.

—Are you sure it works, he asked her, and she said she'd taken it yesterday afternoon deep into the bush at the bottom of the garden and tried it out on a tree stump, and it did.

—I don't suppose there's any hurry now, she said. She took cushions from the sofa, the cushions his mother embroidered with the skill of her youth and another country, and they lay together on the floor wrapped tight in one another's arms. They didn't make love but lay still, waiting for the moment of another consummation. Nor did they speak, they simply held one another, until she said, I am cold, and he said, Perhaps it is time.

—Who will be first? she asked, and he said I must be the one to do it.

He went to a cabinet and took out a bottle of slivovica and two small glasses. They drank with solemn eyes, then they lay down again and he put his arm around her and held her, and put the small round muzzle under her left breast, pressing it into the thin greenish checked fabric of her summer school dress, and she put her fingers over his and pushed against them so they pulled the trigger. He lay for a long time without moving, and then turned the gun around and pressed it into the grey polyester of his own shirt front, but though his fingers tightened several times they did not complete the action. They still lay together thus, she cold and he with the awakening chill of life, a little of her blood upon them both, when his mother came home as always at three o'clock from the cafeteria and screamed out the realisation of her worst fears of this never to cease being foreign country.

◆　　◆　　◆

Emma's mother, the scared-of-burglars possessor of a small enamelled black and ivory pistol a work of art as everything about her must be, would say to her daughter, Emma, why don't you invite your friends around sometime? She would catalogue the possibilities of hospitality: tea, one afternoon, buy some cakes from the patisserie; a pool party with why not a little claret cup suitable for nearly grown girls; a barbecue indeed, marinate some chicken and toast marshmallows. Not she said that I am *au fait* with toasting marshmallows but one reads that they are delicious. After all she said what is the point of sending you across the city to that exclusive—understand but don't say expensive— school if you never bring any of your little friends home?

Mrs Wharton knew that a good school does two things for you: it enables you to say that you have been there, and gives you useful friends for the rest of your life. But the latter not automatically; it needs working at.

Emma said, Oh Mama, but could not explain that school was not manouevrable, you could not suddenly ask people home to tea, or pool parties, or barbecues, there was an etiquette to be observed. Emma was a newcomer; her parents had not seen early enough in her life (the right moment was at birth) their future prosperity, and although she'd been very young when her name was put on the waiting list, by the time she was offered a place the cliques were formed. She was not pushy enough to break into them, nor seductive.

She had another problem: cleverness. A swot she was, quiet, but she knew the answers. A habit not easily forgiven. If only, sighed her mama, she could meet girls on her own ground. Diane Wharton herself hostessed brilliant parties, was a magnificent figure still as thin as in her modelling heydays despite the expensive dining she adored; well, she said, stroking her concave front, I live on my nerves in my business you can't help it it keeps the weight off. Emma was slight and fair and wouldn't command even a first glance in school uniform, but dressed by her mother from her classy boutique—called with costly brevity *Di's*—she could look very striking. So thought her mama, not seeing that her daughter's charm lay not in suddenness but in the reward of contemplation.

Emma sat on the long train journey to school and read; her fair hair combed smooth into a thick plait fell over one shoulder and you could fancy it was its weight that bent her long neck forward over the book; her grey eyes were hooded by heavy round lids and her pale skin unblemished. When you watched her for a while the pure lines and delicate colours of her face gave you an ache in the chest for their beauty. *Too rich for use, for earth too dear*. You could imagine her sitting in just that manner gravely embroidering and looking at the world beyond her tower only in a mirror of beaten silver.

So thought a young man who sat in the train every day with a book of his own and hoped to see her. He got on long before her fashionable suburb, far away where the edge of the city petered out in a rim of cheap and distant housing. He went to a state school, one of the last of the selectives; he was clever too and an ambitious primary school teacher had put him up to it. He read a great deal in English to make up for his background; he had been born in Yugoslavia and was called Novica Cecik.

One day Emma sat opposite him in the train and lowering her eyes began to read. He was transfixed by the high arched domes of her eyelids; he had never imagined that such simple shapes could contain so much loveliness. He looked at them for a long time before he moved his eyes down to her book and saw that it was the same as his, same edition even; he laughed a small chuckle of delight. Enough to draw her eyes up to him.

—I see we are reading the same book, he said.

She smiled and nodded, her eyes wavering back to the page. Nice girls don't speak to young men on trains. But they don't like to be rude.

—Do you like *The Tempest*?

—I think so. I haven't read much of it.

—I think it's tremendous, he said. His English was perfect, it was the only thing that gave him away as a foreigner. He spoke it proudly, forming the words lovingly in his mouth.

—This is the third time I have read it.

Some days later she sat in the only empty seat, next to him.

—I finished *The Tempest*, she said. You were right, it's marvellous.

—O brave new world, that has such people in it, he said, and then blushed in case she thought he meant the words to be as ironic as Miranda's are unintentionally in the play. But she smiled and he wanted to say that he imagined Miranda to be just like her, but was too shy.

After that they often sat or stood together, always with a book in hand, but after a bit they didn't read them, they talked about them. And thus themselves. And then they began to lend each other favourites and talk about them. Novica, a clever boy, was studying mathematics and physics and chemistry; Emma, a clever girl, Latin and French and German. They had one subject in common: English literature.

English literature is about love and sex, and sex and religion, and death and love, and nature and sex, all the important things. They had plenty to talk about. They tasted the heady pleasures of not having to dissemble. They could be as intellectual as they wished. They discovered the sensuality that goes with the intellectual. The long boring train trip to school became far too short.

—Shall I see you home from the train? May I? he asked, his manners as faultless as his grammar.

At first Emma said, Oh no he couldn't possibly, and then she thought why not, and so he began to walk her home through the leafy absent streets; together they dawdled past secret walled gardens and watched the spring blossom in azaleas and flowering almonds and poetic daffodils. At first they stopped at her corner, and then she took him home, leading him past lawns spread with the fleshy shards of magnolia petals into the pretty back sitting-room that was her own place.

For love all love of other sights controls
And make one little room an everywhere

Her mother was always out at the boutique in the next village, as the suburban shopping centres in those parts call themselves, and her father was never home from the city before seven, tired and remote with the rituals of money-making.

They enjoyed the privacy of conversation away from the bored involuntary eavesdroppers of the train, and began to read to one another the wonderful things they'd just discovered. They read Donne and Marvell and the Elizabethans, and took pleasure in teasing their nubile sensualities with explicit love poems, each delicately knowing the other's awareness of what was being said, but not yet openly admitting. It was still Literature. One day he kissed her; cleverness became flesh.

Emma bloomed. Her mother looked at the light in her eye and the curve to her waist and said when are we going to send the invitations to that pool party, and was irritated that still her daughter stalled. And then with that unreliability of parents that makes their children's lives a misery she came home early from the shop.

Emma from the corner of her eye saw the grey Porsche slither round the corner of the house and into its garage. Their situation was not compromising; they were drinking tea and he was reading Donne—*This flea is you and I, and this Our mariage bed and mariage temple is*—and they were laughing slightly ecstatically but hardly improperly. They were not sitting on the windowseat that looked down over the long polished garden to native bush at the bottom, bodies pressed together, kissing and entranced, as they might have been.

Mrs Wharton seeing just her daughter's greenish chequered back through the window thought, Oh bugger, I have forgotten to get in another stock of TV dinners (meals had to be works of art only when she was there to consume them, though a case could have been made for the TV dinner as pop art: bright colours and odd textures in shapely white frames). Oh well, Emma can cook herself some eggs tonight, they're very nourishing. The Whartons were to dine with friends at Le French Café; she adored *nouvelle cuisine*, though her husband preferred a squarer meal.

—Mama, said Emma, her face and manner and the little back sitting-room all composed, this is my friend Novica Cecik. I have brought him home to tea.

In another age Diane Wharton would have called for her vinaigrette and had an attack of the vapours, but lacking at this hour servants and knowing a vinaigrette merely as a dressing for salads she did these things only metaphorically. To the young man she offered a prickly bouquet of fragments of polite phrases: a mangled *how do you do*, a *but surely*, several *I don't know*s, one *not quite proper*, and an *Emma darling* or two but directed still at the boy who bowed possibly under the onslaught but as likely from native elegance until finally her *young man I think you'd better* chased him away with the most exiguous of leave-takings.

Then Diane Wharton became superb. She achieved the moving simplicity of liturgy.

Oh Emma how could you

Oh Emma when we trusted you

Oh Emma what will the neighbours think Oh Emma

Oh Emma a common boy a foreigner oh how could you

Oh Emma after all we've done for you

Oh Emma how could you ungrateful your father and I day and night every advantage how could throw it all away

Oh Emma I cannot bear it

Her voice flew through all the scales of anger to sorrow and back again. Her rhythms, her variations were a *tour de force*. She fell back on the glazed chintz sofa exhausted by her brilliant solo performance.

Emma said, But Mama you're always telling me to invite friends home.

—Friends! Friends! *Girl*friends! Don't you know the difference between a girl and a boy? Oh Emma . . . you haven't . . .

—Mama, of course not. What do you think.

Emma had not expected her mama to admire the straight classical line of Novica's nose or the downy prickle of his cheeks or the way his teeth nipped her bottom lip when he kissed her, but she had thought she would be able to explain him. His mind, his wit, the pleasantness of his character. To explain him in terms of her own happiness, at least; a sincere and passionate daughter expecting a loving parent to understand.

But when her father came home she still had not succeeded.

I do not wish to be an ogre in my child's life, he had said long ago when his wife demanded that he punish his daughter, but his absence from her daily domestic life cast him sometimes in that role; he tried to counterbalance it by being the most sugary of daddies. Neither connection made for much intimacy. He loved his daughter dearly, but nobody noticed.

—What's this chap's name?

—Novica Cecik, said Emma.

—Noveetsa Seesick! shrieked Mrs Wharton. The spiky foreign name filled her mouth, tangling in her expensive dentistry and pressing against her uvular until she thought she might puke.

—He's very clever, Papa. You've got to be brilliant to get into that school, it's much more difficult than private schools.

Her father said, Well, if he's clever, remembering as he was not supposed to that his father had had a dusty corner shop in a western suburb and that the clever boy he had been had climbed to his present high panelled office overlooking the Opera House by means of scholarships and prizes . . . He could be quite a nice boy, Diane, after all—

—What does his father do, said Mama, inexorably.

—He's a gardener. He works for the shire council. And his mother works in a cafeteria doing lunches, and he's got four brothers and sisters and lives in a little wooden house in a dreadful dreary suburb and he's the most interesting person I know.

Thus counterattacking by confirming her mama's worst fears, Emma burst into tears and went to bed. Mrs Wharton was almost too upset to go to Le French Cafe but made a brave effort.

Next day in the train Emma her eyes large with tears that like a convex glass held misery trapped inside said, We are not supposed to see one another ever again. My mother . . .

There were no words for her mother.

Emma said, She'd stop me catching the train if there were any other way for me to go to school. She's working on that.

Mrs Wharton rang up to make sure her daughter was home at precisely the right time, and turned up in person to make sure she was alone. Emma always was. But not always from school; she and Novica played truant. She went down the hill to the station as usual, but caught a train the other way. He met her; they walked slowly through the scruffy streets to give his mother and the other children time to get out of the house, then spent the day together. She caught an afternoon train back and dawdled up the hill and home on schedule.

They didn't do it very often, hardly once a week, though several times they took two days off running to make their absences seem more logical. Emma typed out notes on her mother's typewriter for a variety of malaises: heavy colds, viral infections, influenzas, gastric attacks, a poisoned toe. She signed them with a practised imitation of her mother's violent ink flourish. Novica had always written his own absence notes anyway.

They read *Romeo and Juliet*. The similarity of their situations sent shivers down their spines. *Oh she doth teach the torches to burn bright*, he whispered to her tremulous intent face. They left behind *The Tempest* and Miranda's unbroken virgin knot and found their own truth in the consummated passion of the lovers of Verona. They lacked a kindly priest to bless but made their own vows. They were so perfectly happy that their previous lives, before they had known one another, became impossible to imagine.

—It's like being a butterfly, said Emma, her hair falling like silvery striped wings over her naked shoulders. You can't possibly remember the awful feeble worm you've changed out of.

—And you can't possibly change back into it, said Novica.

They knew the dangers of getting pregnant and took precautions. That didn't catch them. The nosiness of her exclusive private school did. Being seen to keep a sharp eye on the welfare of its students, Emma's pastoral tutor rang up Mrs Wharton at the shop to express concern at the girl's poor health, it did seem to be affecting her work, her grades were not at all what they had been.

This time her mother had no words. The virtuoso performance of the tea party had left nothing for this horror. Through the thin lips of fury she said, The boarding house for you my girl. As soon as they can take you. We'll see how you manage to go whoring about then.

—It's fixed for Sunday afternoon, said Emma to Novica on Wednesday.

—And just make sure my girl you're at school till then. Any more truancy and I'll take a stick to you, old as you are.

—It was true, about being a butterfly, said Emma. A beautiful life for a day and now it's over. You can't stop being a butterfly, but you can't keep it up either. Oh Novica, I can't go to boarding school and never see you, I'd rather die.

Metaphor. Hyperbole. But gradually they felt the literalness. The publicity of the train bound them tighter in their misery, in the pain of sitting contained and quiet and not touching one another. All the springs of their joy and wit turned to bitter salty tears and their bodies ached with the effort of not shedding them.

On Thursday Emma brought *Romeo and Juliet* to the train. They read the last scene.

> *Oh here*
> *Will I set up my everlasting rest*
> *And shake the yoke of inauspicious stars*
> *From this world-wearied flesh.*

—My mother's got a little gun, said Emma. I'll bring it to your place, tomorrow, as usual.

❖   ❖   ❖

Suicide Pact, the headlines sang. Boy Lover Claims Suicide Pact. Suicide Pact Failure Tragedy. I Should Have Died Too Says Boy Over Slain Sweetheart.

Boy 17 Remanded Children's Court Boy Charged Murder Schoolgirl Lover

No names, they were too young.

❖   ❖   ❖

Diane Wharton did not see how her life could go on after her daughter's death. I do not know how I will survive, she said. It was true, she did not know, but survival is not something you need to know how to do, it happens unless you deliberately take steps to avoid it. So Mrs Wharton survived.

She said, How lucky I am to have my little shop. If I could not throw myself into my work where would I be?

Occasionally in the supermarket she would think of buying some TV dinners and then cruelly remember that there was no longer any call for them. Then she would hurry to the continental section and deliberate the choosing of some distracting delicacy; a pot of goose-liver, perhaps, or a truffle in a tin, or some rosy lobster bisque.

Mr Wharton who had his work too and was already immersed in it without finding much relief went to see Novica because he wanted to understand. He felt old and weak and grey, grey to look at and grey in looking. His wife took comfort in blame; the guilt was the boy's; the foolish daughter . . . there she stopped thinking, sanity saved by not dwelling, went back to punishing the guilty. All the boy's fault. Mr Wharton was glad for her comfort, but couldn't share it; it made no sense, and he believed that everything could be made sense of, it was his ability to make it that had raised him to that high office whose thick carpets and brilliant collection of modern art pretended that it wasn't a centre for manipulating things and people.

He found Novica beyond manipulation, and not much help in making sense.

— He didn't know, he told his wife, this beauty that his brains had won. Kept saying that he didn't understand why he didn't . . . kept asking—not me, himself, was he a coward. Said something about destroying the perfect beauty of their act, and now all he can do is stay alive and mourn her forever. Bereft. Terribly romantic, the way he talked, but you couldn't get away from its sincerity. Poor kid, his life's gone as much as Emma's . . . he really loved her, you know. They really were in love. Poor kids.

— I don't think talking about it does any good, said Mrs Wharton.

With dry fingers she stuck a spine of false lashes to the rim of each high-domed eyelid, and coloured above it with violet shadow. They were going to the Pavilion du Parc that night. An old favourite.

Neighbourhood
Fortress

*W*hen they give me the case of Donna Pilger's suicide I know why. Two reasons, both obvious. She's a woman, and the matter is in no doubt. The investigation is just a formality.

'I'm sending Senior Constable Phil Murphy,' I hear the boss say to the bereaved husband on the phone. 'He's pretty upset,' he tells me. 'You'll know how to handle things.'

In the car I read the history. Donna Pilger shut herself in her house and shot herself. Left a note. *I cannot go on like this any longer. Darling, I know you'll understand.* All very straightforward. Sad, but clear.

The house in a middling suburb is middling too. Comfortable, not affluent. Double-fronted cream brick veneer, small and rather low, very neatly kept. Colourful beds of flowers, that kind of thing, where the other houses in the street go in more for shrubs and lawn. At the back, a garage of the tin shed variety. And all over the place the green and white stickers of Neighbourhood Watch.

Noel Pilger looks at me. 'Oh, I expected a man.' There is a faint flicker in his eyes as he says this. Is it relief? Steady on Philly, I say to myself. Don't go getting paranoid. Not all men think a woman is a soft cop. Why not simple surprise? 'The name. Phil,' he goes on.

'Philomena,' I say, as always. Philomena's a great name, I think my mum showed great taste, but it's not easy.

He nods. 'Come in.'

The inside of the house is pleasant as the outside. Nothing flash. Estapolled pine floorboards, several oriental carpets, a fawn velvet lounge suite, table and chairs in that teak stuff, Parker, I think it is, that a few years ago used to be called contemporary. Stereo, telly, video.

But first, the front door. It clanks like a fortress. Solid chain, double deadlocks. 'I could do without all this,' says Noel. 'I'm dead scared I'm going to lock myself out.'

'Not your idea then.'

'No. My wife's. She was nervous. Scared of burglars, people getting in. She liked to feel safe.'

There are not only deadlocks on the doors and windows, there's a burglar alarm too. Electronic tape snakes round all the windows and doors. Noel shows me how the system works.

'The switch is in that cupboard at the end of the passage. You have to check that all the windows and doors are shut . . .'

'The alarm's linked to every one?' I actually know all this. It's in the original report.

'Yes. No exceptions. After all, what would be the point? So you turn on the alarm and you've got forty seconds to get out the front door. Same when you come home. You unlock the door and soon's it opens you've got forty seconds to get to the switch and turn it off. Bit of a sprint sometimes,' he says mournfully.

'So your wife was inside, locked in, when . . .'

'Mm. I came home and the place was shut up. Nothing unusual in that, as I say, my wife was nervous. I get out m'key, open up, ready to do the sprint, and the door sticks. Only goes a couple of inches. The chain's on. The forty seconds passes, and thar she blows. Goes on screaming away, no stopping her. Brought out the whole neighbourhood. And the police, of course.'

'So the police were with you when you found . . .'

He grimaces. 'Mm.'

'Lying on the floor in the lounge, the gun beside her hand.'

He nods.

'Maybe it was one of those burglars she was so scared of, he got in, she surprised him, he shot her and scarpered without taking anything.'

He shakes his head. 'Not possible. Even if he could've got in, he couldn't've got out. Even if he knew how to set the alarm, and had the keys so he could lock the front door—and it has to be the front door, doesn't work on the back, or the windows— he couldn't've put the chain on, see?'

Do I detect a faint note of triumph in his voice?

'So if somebody else shot her, he—she—would've had to be still in the house when you and the police got in?'

Again, I wonder about the triumph.

'I imagine that didn't happen,' he says, sarcastic.

'What about the gun?'

'It was hers. She liked to have it round. Same reason as the locks. I thought she'd handed it in. With those new gun laws. I asked her had she, she said yes.'

'She lied to you.'

'Mm.'

A neurotic woman. Nervous. So nervous she breaks the law to keep a gun to protect her. The picture fits.

Or does it? Is shooting herself in the head likely behaviour for a nervous woman? Wouldn't she be equally nervous of guns? Does a woman paranoid about violence act with violence against herself?

You need to be a psychiatrist in this job . . .

Just keep thinking, Philomena Murphy.

I look about the house. Setting up the burglar alarm would have cost more than the place is worth. I'm too polite to say this, though. I remark on the carpets instead.

'I suppose they'd be pretty valuable.'

We're in the kitchen. There's rather a nice specimen, not too small, in front of the sink.

'Doesn't it get grotty, with all the washing up?'

'Oh no. Not at all. Anyway, they're tough, these rugs, the nomads use them in the desert. Let their camels walk on them. This is very comfortable to stand on. Good for the feet.'

I bend over to stroke it. I like the feel of oriental carpets. I'm planning to buy one.

'You like carpets? There's a good one in here.' He takes me into the lounge. I look at the diagram where the body was. She thoughtfully didn't do it where she'd mess anything up. Not like some suicides, who try to make things as ugly as possible for those who find them.

The carpet under the coffee table is a goldy colour, with red and blue bands of pattern. It's got quite a nice silky feel.

'You were at work when it happened?'

'I suppose so. Though I might have left. I left a bit early. Went to David Jones and bought a bottle of wine. It's good there, and quite cheap.'

'A special celebration?'

'Oh no. Just a little treat. Just, you know . . .' He turns away, his hand over his eyes. He holds himself very tense for a minute, I can see his funny bone quiver, and then turns back. His eyes are full of tears. 'It gets a bit lonely, a woman on her own in the house all day. A little treat . . . it used to cheer her up.'

There are lots of flowers in the house. They stop you noticing that the decoration is rather dull, sort of safe, all cream paint and curtains and those soothing seascape pictures. But the flowers are marvellous, great bowls of them, scented and glowing. Fresh and full of life, when the woman who put them there . . .

In the dining-room there's a bookcase, full of books of all shapes and sizes. They're all about wine. Every single one of them.

'I see you're interested in wine.'

'I'd like to be. I like to read about it, anyway.'

'Do you have a, what, a collection? A cellar?'

'Ah. Chance would be a fine thing.' He points to a tall package on the table, in the familiar houndstooth wrapping. 'I'm afraid it's just the odd bottle. David Jones, or Farmers. Depending on what's a good price.'

We go into a spare room which seems to have been Donna Pilger's sewing room. There's a large table with a machine at one end, a mug of pens and pencils at the other. An ironing board, and across it a dress, partly pinned together. Cupboards and drawers, and another set of bookshelves. The titles here are nearly all Mills and Boon. I suddenly feel sad. I reckon if she expected life to be like a Mills and Boon it's no wonder she gave up.

The bedroom's pretty dull, too, very tasteful and tidy. On the dressing-table are a lot of little bowls and vases and dishes, fine white china with pale blue painted flowers. Noel picks one up. 'She loved these. I used to give them to her for Christmas and birthdays. She couldn't get enough of them.'

I don't know why I'm keeping on with this. As the boss said, the case is straightforward. Nobody could've got out of this house. It has to be suicide. Nevertheless, I make the rounds with this sad man. Walk through the house. Examine the impregnable windows. The back door. More double deadlocks. Outside, a terrace, with three shallow steps down to a neat back garden. Rows of vegetables. A barbecue.

The door of the garage is open. Inside there's a white Laser parked, the usual odds and ends of junk that families accumulate, and a quantity of gardening tools. On a shelf is a pile of empty chocolate boxes, a box of newspapers, and another half full of bottles. Looks like Donna was the recycling type.

'I guess that's some of the odd bottles.'

'Oh, over a period of time,' he says, and when I look, they're pretty old, all covered with dust, how thick you can see by the fingerprints around the necks. And the labels are quite eaten away, though I can make out 1966 on one. Old, all right. Nearly as old as me.

'Looks like you've got silverfish, or mice,' I say.

'Place's full of pests. Donna didn't like using pesticides or poisons and such. Watch out for the redbacks.'

We go back inside. 'Well, it's all pretty straightforward, Noel,' I say. 'Just routine. A few more enquiries, just for the record, and we'll leave you alone.'

'More enquiries?' He looks irritated. 'What more can there be?'

'Oh, talk to the neighbours . . . just tidying, really.'

I have to wait until the evening to catch the neighbours. Men and women both work about here. Nobody's seen anything between three and five on Tuesday afternoon. What about kids? They're at after school care, or off with friends, nobody's admitting to latchkey children. Nobody knows the Pilgers anyway. Pleasant people, kept themselves to themselves. Already past tense. They believe she spent a lot of time in the garden. Smart deduction, this. No, they didn't really speak to them. You know how it is.

'What about Neighbourhood Watch?' I point to the green and white sticker on the front door.

Oh, they scratch the numbers on videos and TVs, bikes and things.

Not notice anything suspicous at number fifteen on Tuesday afternoon.

What do I know about Donna Pilger? That she's forty-six, has a daughter working as a children's nanny in England, that she sews and gardens quite extensively, that she's paranoid about burglars, that her husband brings her little treats to cheer her up. I ask Noel to let me look through the photograph album. There she is, young, with her baby daughter, looking very pretty. She has a round face, with large features, big eyes and far apart, a wide smiling mouth. A photogenic face. There it is through the years, smiling at the camera. Happily? Or just photogenically? The most recent is several years old; she's standing by a blossoming May bush, holding a great bundle of its branches in her arms, like a parody of a bridal bouquet. Grinning with delight. Laughing at herself, with a slight gleeful shrug of her shoulders. Isn't she?

'Your wife was a beautiful woman,' I say to Noel.

'Mm.' He turns away again. I realise I've been tactless. Where's my female sympathy now?

'I'm sorry,' I say. My eyes fill with tears too. Imagine what a blow the loss of this dear smiling woman would be.

When I get back to the station the boss is annoyed. 'What the hell do you think you're doing,' he screams, 'treating the man like suspect number one. God, Philly, the whole bloody thing was a formality.'

'I wanted to be sure . . .'

'Playing detective is what you're at. Slobbering around like a bloodhound. You read the notes. Cut and dried. Cut and dried.' He splutters to a stop.

Formality, I think. Cut and dried.

Next day I drive to Pilger's place of work. It's in one of those minor industrial areas, a small factory making Hang-Rite filing cabinet fittings. I go in my own time, in my own clothes. I wait outside in my own car until I see him leave.

There's a small room with a secretary, receptionist, whatever, Miss Havas a little plaque says her name is, and behind her a door, half-open, into what must be Pilger's office; I can see the end of a desk, a mess of papers. I dredge my brain for anything about filing cabinets to make intelligent conversation with. End up opting for ignorance so she can tell me. She beckons me to a tomato red job, stands beside me, pulling out drawers, explaining the systems. Her breath smells of wine. At eleven in the morning? Is she an alcoholic? Doesn't look the type. Maybe it's the dreariness of filing cabinets all day. Now, through the door into Pilger's office I can see a wine bottle standing beside two tall-stemmed glasses, whose bowls are the heavy perfect ovals of teardrops, not crystal clear but puddled with dregs and the greasy touch of lips and fingers. Glasses of that quality don't come cheap.

I look at the young woman explaining the hangers to me. Young is what she mainly is. She's got brown hair in a pony tail, and her figure is not exactly dumpy but not graceful. Her skin is very fine, pink and white. Her fingers slide across the files as though giving and receiving pleasure. I watch them. On her right hand a large sapphire ring refracts the light as her fingers move across the files. I bet she's vain about those hands. Likes to watch them. See the sapphire flash in its circlet of pearls.

'So,' she says, 'which kind? Do you think you'll need?'

When I say I don't know she blushes. You can see the warm blood flow in a tide up her face; it's fascinating, I've never seen anyone blush so transparently before. She sighs and I smell the wine on her breath again. A push shuts the drawer with its own weight.

'I'd better talk to my colleague,' I say, and nod and smile and hurry off.

Think, Philomena Murphy. Think.

When I next report to the station the boss is furious again, calmed down cold furious, not raging.

'Well, Nancy Drewe,' he says, dripping sarcasm.

Nancy Drewe?

'Ever heard of ethics? Proper behaviour for a police officer, on and off duty?'

I act innocent. Well, I feel pretty innocent.

'Another phone call from Pilger. He claims you're hounding him.'

'I was just looking at filing cabinets.' My random thoughts begin to crystallise. How did Pilger know I was at his office today? He didn't see me. Surely I don't shriek cop even out of uniform? Ha. He's acting like a guilty man. The geezer doth protest too much, methinks. I've felt it all along. Sort of.

'The bloke loses his wife in tragic circumstances and the *police*,' (very nasty the way he spits this out) 'the *police* hound him. Unethically.'

'He said that? The hounding?' The boss nods. 'I reckon,'

—I'm saying this before I know I'm going to—'I reckon our Mr Pilger has just committed the perfect crime.'

'The perfect . . .? Come on, Philly. You've been reading too many thrillers.'

'I never read detective stories.' My voice comes out a bit prim.

'Okay. The perfect crime.' Heavy humouring. 'How?'

'I dunno. But it would be, wouldn't it. That fortress of a house. Absolutely impregnable, from the *inside*—and why, by the way? Because, he says, his wife is nervous. Anyway, that impregnable house, and the only person who could have made it so having to be the person still inside, having to be the dead woman, who shut herself in, doors and windows locked, chain across, alarm on—again, why? Still scared of burglars, even over her dead body? So she shuts herself in and shoots herself. Doesn't make sense.'

'Maybe. Still makes more sense than anything else.'

'Not if there's another way out.'

'Where? Up the chimney? An anti-Santa Claus? Through the manhole and into the roof, off with a couple of tiles, jump down into the garden and off across the back fences?' He chuckles at the wit of this.

I shake my head. 'No fireplace. And the roof's tin, or sheets of something. No ladder at the manhole.'

'You looked?' He blows out air like a wind cherub. 'Leave it, Philly. It's suicide. Remember the note? Normal people always find suicide incomprehensible. You just don't want to believe it, that's all. The facts, Philly.'

So much for thinking, Philomena Murphy.

He piles on the work. I don't even have time to think about thinking. Every now and then I see the smiling face of Donna Pilger among the town's crowds, until I look sharply and it's another woman altogether.

205

The inquest plumps for suicide. Well, it would, on that evidence.

Several weeks pass. The boss calls me in. 'You've got a visitor. No funny business, mind.' A middle-aged woman, thin, sunburnt, holding on to her handbag as though it's her life and she expects it to be stolen. She's called Janice Adams, and she's best friend of Donna Pilger.

'I wanted to talk to you. They said you investigated. I've tried and tried and I don't understand. I don't believe it. Donna wouldn't have done that.'

Classic best friend behaviour.

'Do you know the circumstances?'

'Yes I do. All of them. The locks and the chain and the burglar alarm. I know. But if you knew Donna you'd see the impossible bit was her shooting herself.'

'Maybe there was more despair than . . .'

'Donna never had a gun. Wouldn't know what to do with a gun. And all that burglar alarm business. She hated it. Course, she didn't say anything to Noel, didn't want to hurt his feelings him being so keen to have it, but left to herself she'd never have bothered to shut the doors even.'

All the melted-away little niggles of thought crystallise again, sharp as ice.

Janice goes on. 'I know she wouldn't have killed herself. She was enjoying life too much. She'd just started a *career*! As a writer!'

'A writer?'

'Yup. Sold two stories to the *Women's Weekly*, and one to *Woman's Day*. Thrilled to bits she was, when she saw them in print. And she was writing a Mills and Boon. Sent away and got those outlines they give you. She was up to the last chapter, she said.'

'Did her husband know about this?'

'Oh yes. He thought it was nice for her to have something to do. With him being away so much.'

'Away?'

'Oh, just at nights, weekends sometimes. Those wine clubs of his, always meetings, conferences. Took up all his spare time. Donna wasn't very interested. She'd have a glass of wine with a meal, and that, but she couldn't really see what the fuss was about.'

Janice holds tight to her handbag. 'Donna didn't mind, really, him not being there. She had her gardening, and dress-making, and her writing. "You sure it's wine that takes him out so much?" I said to her. "Maybe it's another woman." After all, if your friends don't warn you, who will? But she just smiled, that lovely big smile of hers. Come to think of it, she didn't say anything. I don't know what she thought.'

'Did you really think there was another woman?'

'Well, not for certain. Could have been. But there was a lot of wine too. He bought it by the case load. Always had. But it was only in the last couple of years it took him away so much.'

Think, Philomena Murphy, think.

The bottle of wine to cheer a wife up.

The secretary's sensuous fingers.

The double-fronted cream brick veneer, so safely decorated. The neat flat garden with its beds of flowers. Of vegetables. The terrace. The garage with the Laser. The boxes of newspapers and empty wine bottles.

'Have you got copies of those *Women's Weekly* stories?'

I go round to Janice's place and get them. In my own time, of course. I want to see what they'll tell me about Donna Pilger. She didn't use her own name, but called herself Lucinda Darcy;

I wonder if Janice Adams is maybe making it all up; there's no guarantee that Donna actually wrote these stories. This Lucinda person could be anybody.

They're the typical magazine story: man/woman, boy/girl, troubles but they really love each other, happy ever after. I think maybe they're rather well written, quite a nice turn of phrase in fact. The last one is quite gripping. It's about a middle-aged man who had a fling before he ever met his wife, and the woman turns up with this kid he's never known about, who's a teenager now, and she blackmails him. She'll tell his wife if he doesn't cough up. This makes his life a misery, he can't stand it, he decides the only way is to confess all to his wife. He sits beside her on the settee. He takes her hand and looks into her eyes and speaks in a soft loving voice. I cannot go on like this any longer, he says. Darling I know you'll understand. Of course she does, all's sorted out, happy ever after.

Yes, I think, if Donna Pilger was Lucinda Darcy she wasn't at all a bad writer. Janice has got a point about the career . . .

Oh my God. Think, Philomena. And all those little crystallisings of thought turn into one big sharp icicle pointing at the truth.

'I need a search warrant,' I tell the boss.

'No way,' he says. He won't even listen. 'Suicide, girlie, suicide. Coroner said. Case is closed.'

I drive to the pleasant suburb and park round the corner. The houses rest in midday peace. In the Pilger garden the flowers are dying, their tall glossy heads bend and brown. I walk down the driveway. Peer about. No neighbourhood watching. Past the garage, the bedraggled vegetable beds, up the shallow steps to the terrace. I've got a brick wrapped in newspaper in a string bag. I heave it through the laundry window. The siren sings.

Quick with the catch, push on the frame, heave up on to the sill, in. The siren screams. Into the kitchen. The oriental carpet is still in front of the sink. I peel it back, and find what I'm looking for.

I sit and wait for my colleagues to come.

❖   ❖   ❖

'It was the carpet,' I say, 'and the winebottles.' They are all standing around me with this-had-better-be-good looks on their faces. Mixed with   pity-to-end-a-promising-career-like-this   pious frowns. 'Look at it. It's superb. It's not at all the kind of cheap nomadic rug people put in their kitchens. I know, I've been doing a bit of research, because I'm going to buy one. Whereas this rug . . .' I drag them into the living room 'is Kashmiri, made in Pakistan, pretty, feels nice, but not a patch on the one in the kitchen. Pilger would have known that, it's elementary, but he lied about it. He was very keen I not look at the carpet in the kitchen. I knew that at the time, but not why. It was one of the things that worried me.

'Then there were the bottles.' I take them out to the garage. 'Pilger said he only ever bought the odd bottle. He said he didn't have a cellar, but those bottles came out of a cellar. Look at the dust. It's slow ancient dust. And the fingermarks. They've been handled *after* that dust got on them. And they've had their labels eaten. Mice or silverfish or snails, whatever; the cellar isn't vermin proof. But even so, you can read some of the labels.' *rang Herm, yrrel Pin, Rou om*, and there's a speckled picture of a man with a basket of grapes on his back. 'Wine I don't know anything about, the names don't mean anything, but look at that date. 1966. You don't need to be a connoisseur to know a wine as old as that would cost a fortune. Unless you bought it when it was young and kept it in a cellar until it was ready.

Janice Adams said Pilger had always bought cases of wine. So, more lies. Pilger had a cellar, but he denied it.

'Anyway, it wasn't till I found out that the suicide note was a fake that I was certain. Remember what it looked like? You think, a torn and scrappy bit of lined paper, she just grabbed what she could, poor woman, it's another sign of her despair. In fact, Pilger tore it out of a manuscript. I reckon you won't find that, he'd have destroyed it. But here it is.' I hold out the magazine. '*Sing Like a Bird* the story's called, and here, near the end: *I cannot go on like this any longer. Darling, I know you'll understand.*

'There's the cellar.' I lift back the carpet. This time it's easier, the strong adhesive tape has lost some of its stick. In the wooden floorboards there's a trapdoor cut. My colleagues try, but can't lever it up. They cast smug that's-blown-it looks on me. 'That's one of those building inspection trapdoors. Usually they're hidden under lino tiles, or cork, and usually they're nailed down. Not this one. I reckon this one's probably screwed in, from underneath.

'Look, here's the scenario. Pilger shoots his wife, tidily, in the lounge-room. She's fond of him, she likes him, she wouldn't be suspicious. He locks the doors and windows, sets the alarm. Which isn't his wife's idea, it's his, and I reckon all part of a long-term plan to do away with her. Climbs down through the trapdoor, closes the lid with the carpet stuck to it with double-sided tape. Fastens it in place. Not much room under there, the house is only a couple of feet off the ground, but okay for a cellar, cool, though a bit verminous. Best somebody in Pilger's reasonably modest circumstances can hope for, and certainly lots of space for wine. Has to crawl, wriggle on his stomach even, across to the side of the house.' I drag them all off again and point out the customary little door that gives access to under the house. It's got a shining brass padlock. 'That bed of delphiniums would have hidden it from the street quite nicely. So, the impossible achieved, the impregnable fortress breached. The perfect crime committed.' I look at the boss, who looks away.

'I reckon you'd find, after a bit, after a decent interval, the inconsolable widower marries the nice little Miss Havas, who shifts her fine sapphire ring to her left hand, and they drink wine together happily ever after.'

Of course I'm in strife. You don't heave bricks through windows and get away with it. Is this the end of the glorious criminal-catching career of Philomena Murphy? But there's a bit of glory, too. I did uncover a murderer.

Janice Adams has found the manuscript of the Mills and Boon. All but finished; the last chapter needs a bit of work. She's going to fix it, send it off. She says it's brilliant, they're sure to publish it.

The
Ice-cream
Bursts

I *shan't be able to resist it. I know*
I shan't. It's too seductive. The call of the void. I can feel it pulling
me, pulling me over. I shall have to jump. I know I won't be able
to prevent myself.

On the fourth day of the Festivale Estivale these words were
repeated by a large number of people. They'd originally been
spoken on the first day of the festival by Bianca Madin, and
referred to the Hotel Hierophant where the writers were staying.
It was a very grand place, much grander than most of them
were used to, though they were glad of the practice, with acres
of marble foyers and squads of minions to carry luggage and
messages. It was built in the form of what is called an atrium:
fourteen floors of guest accommodation surrounding and looking
down on a classy cafe on a lower level. Each room opened
on to a kind of balcony passage, with a chest-high wall,

overlooking the cafe below. Bianca had emerged from the lift on the twelfth floor, dressed as always in one of her billowing caftans, in yellow this time, with ropes of amber beads and a number of topaz rings that shattered the light in the wake of her extravagant gestures. She'd walked to the edge of the balcony, stood on tiptoe, peered over, shuddered, stepped gingerly back on her stiletto-heeled shoes, laid one hand on the balustrade and the other on her heart, and spoken these sentences: *I shall have to jump, I shan't be able to resist*, and so on. Her old friend, the distinguished critic Rupert Chapel, Paulette the hotel trainee who was showing her to her room, and Kate Szabo, who happened to be passing, had all heard her. Rupert had protested: 'Oh my dear, never say it!'

But she had. She'd gone on saying it. Bianca Madin was not one to waste a well-turned idea. In the coffee shop, in the bar, at dinners with publishers, she had repeated her variations on this theme. *It's like cliffs*, she said. *Never let me near a cliff. Always that irresistible urge to go over. To imagine is to do, where I am concerned.* This was a blue day, a cerulean caftan with painted Mexican beads and rings of lapis lazuli on every finger. Bevan Sands, who published her books, said with a certain nervousness: 'But Bianca. You never have. Jumped. Have you?'

'No, I don't seem to have, do I? But that atrium. Never have I felt such a powerful . . .' Her hands fluttered about her head. Somebody mentioned darting kingfisher fingers.

'Promise me,' said Bevan, 'that you will keep well away from the edge.'

On the morning of the third day, Kate Szabo stood looking over the balcony. Large hoops of some sort of metal hung from the glasshouse roof of the atrium and through them were threaded great swathes of fabric, gold and white, which looped down to other hoops on the walls above the cafe. She stared down at the tiny tables, the blobs of people, the general sparkle of glass and cutlery, the shining black harp-shaped surface of the grand piano.

'You can see the power of it. What Bianca means,' said a voice behind her. It was Amanda Warren, a publisher's minder, who'd come to collect Bianca Madin for the morning session, at which she'd be performing: reading from her new novel *Anteroom to a Cage*, which was to be launched on the following day. One quick-off-the-mark reviewer had already hailed it as even more of a *tour de force* than we have grown accustomed to from this writer, and especially admired its pellucid power.

That evening, about 9.30 on the third day of the festival, Bianca Madin went over the edge of the balcony outside her room and plummeted the twelve stories to the cafe below. She caught in one of the swathes of glittering fabric as she went, but it was too flimsy to hold her. Several diners looked up and saw her golden caftan billowing as she fell and thought for the split of a second that she was part of the entertainment. Because of the colour co-ordination. When she landed on the grand piano it became apparent that she wasn't. Bianca Madin had never been a slender person, witness the voluminous caftans. Her landing on the grand piano was not a dining experience that anyone would want to repeat. 'They're just lucky she didn't land on any of them,' said Sergeant Pryor. 'A missile like that. You wouldn't survive.'

So Bianca's words about the irresistibility of high places were on everybody's lips on the fourth day of the Festivale Estivale, when people met as usual in the bar at The Sauce Factory, the arts centre where the festival was being held. Sergeant Pryor needed statements from all the participants. 'Just routine,' he said. The Hierophant was no longer keen to offer its premises. Writers, it seemed, did not behave well.

'It's appallingly inconsiderate,' said the manager, looking at the mess in the cafe. Everybody felt a tinge of guilt, for they'd all heard her remarks and dismissed them, as part of her famous conversation, her wonderful extravagant way with words. They sat drinking coffee and feeling shocked that she should have made them come true. Except Amanda, who was distraught. She entirely blamed herself. She was Bianca's minder, she should have stopped it happening. People telling her that she had done her job properly in every respect, delivering her charge to her room at nine o'clock for an early night as she had required, festivals were so wearing, didn't console her at all. She should have cared for her more carefully.

Bianca's old friend Rupert sat with tears running down his cheeks. 'It's not just the loss of a friend,' he mourned, 'it's the loss of all she might have done. I think she was potentially the greatest writer Australia has produced. Each new thing she did was even more marvellous than the last. Such creative genius. Such fecundity. She never repeated herself.'

'He's writing her obituary,' said Frank Downard to Kate. In the manner of literary festivals, they'd found themselves often together during the last days, beginning over the rather acid bubbly at the opening reception.

'What are you doing here?' Frank had asked her in quite a sexy chatting-up way. He was younger than most of the participants, close to her age. His hair black and curling, his eyes the colour of golden syrup, looking her up and down.

'Me? I'm a groupie,' said Kate, with as bold an eye as he. 'I'm a literary hanger-on.'

'I see,' he said. 'Do you sleep with the performers?'

'Depends on their performance.'

After a bit it turned out that Kate had read Frank's stories in *Southerly* and *Island*, and he'd read hers in *Westerly* and *Meanjin*.

They admired one another's work, they said. 'Have you written a novel?' asked Kate.

'Oh yes,' he replied.

'Found a publisher yet?'

Frank frowned, and looked very black, and Kate knew better than to press. After a moment he said, 'And you?'

'Oh,' she sighed, 'ditto, ditto, ditto.'

'Sing ditto, sing ditto, sing ditto,' and he did sing it, mournfully, to Arthur Sullivan's plaintive tune, which made her laugh.

After that they often met at readings or over lunchtime beers at the bar, the Dead Horse Bar it was called, though really it was just part of the large space of the foyer with tables and a counter for drinks. Not even an espresso machine, complained Frank.

Now they were sitting there together in the gloomy company of the other writers of the Festivale. Papers and readings were cancelled, out of respect.

'Do you think she did commit suicide?' asked Kate.

Frank looked at her, his golden eyes bright.

'Well, I don't know about suicide. But there seems to be no doubt she killed herself. In the grasp of an irresistible desire.'

'Do you really believe that?'

'She said it often enough. We all heard her. Quite wearisome I found her repetition of the theme.'

'We heard her, but none of us thought she meant it.'

'But surely, Kate, you looked over that edge. Didn't you feel the pull of the void?'

'Oh yes. I looked over the edge. I felt the pull. I imagined jumping over, twirling down through those stupid great swags of cloth and landing splat on some surprised cafe patrons. Though I didn't quite envisage wiping out a grand piano. I have the same fantasy when I stand on cliffs. But I don't do it. I never will do it.'

'Well. The fair Bianca did.'

'Mm,' said Kate. 'Of course, if she did do it, it was an act of appalling bad taste. Splattering your innards all over people's dinners like that. If people are going to kill themselves, they should do it privately.'

'Perhaps the mess was a kind of revenge. Suicide as revenge.'

'Revenge? For what? Fame, money, critical acclaim?'

'Okay, all right, but I still reckon the last thing a suicide thinks of is being tidy about it.'

'It's not just the untidiness. It's the grossness. Bianca was a woman who liked to look beautiful; she took enormous trouble over it. Those caftans were gorgeous, in their way, and think of the jewellery. The make-up. I don't reckon she'd have chosen such an *ugly* end. Composed on a bier with hands folded across her chest and sheaves of lilies is more her style.'

'Kate, my little gumshoe, I think you are entirely failing to understand the mentality of a suicide.'

'I'm not considering the mentality of a suicide. I'm considering the mentality of Bianca Madin.'

'Do you think he is?' Frank gestured at a closed door. Sergeant Pryor was interviewing people one by one in the small Rosella Theatre. Everybody responded in much the same way, with Bianca's *bons mots* on her need to jump over the balcony, with sorrow at her loss, and disbelief, plus the rather pointless guilt of failing to do something about it.

'What the hell could they have done,' the sergeant muttered to his constable. 'Tie her to the bed post? The woman was a free agent.'

After her turn at questioning, a small woman carrying a heavy bag of books came with her cup of coffee and sat at Frank and Kate's table. 'Do you mind if I sit here,' she asked. Both felt like saying, yes, we do, but she was already perched on the chair and neither was quite rude enough. Besides, you had to be careful at festivals that you didn't inadvertently offend some very distinguished figure, though it seemed unlikely in this case.

'This is a terrible loss,' she said: avidly was the word that came to both writers' minds. 'Such a brilliant author. So inventive. I couldn't wait for each new book, to see what she'd do next.'

'She got them out quite fast,' said Kate.

'Not fast enough for me,' said the woman. 'I couldn't get enough. I was going to get her to sign these,' she indicated the large bag of books, 'and now it's too late.' She gave a snuffle. 'You know, it's hard to believe she'd do a thing like that. It just shows you what a sensitive person can be pushed to.'

Kate stirred up the sludge in her coffee cup. Frank leaned his head back and studied the pointed lattice arches that defined the ceiling. Sensing that she was stuck with a monologue the woman looked at Kate and Frank. 'Are you authors?'

'No,' they said together.

'Oh.' There was silence. She eyed her books. 'I love *Vile Jelly* the best,' she said. 'I think that's her masterpiece.'

'*The Ice-cream Bursts*,' said Frank.

'*Call Him Soft Names*,' said Kate.

'Rubbish. *The Ice-cream Bursts*.'

'Are you mad?' said Kate. *Call Him Soft Names* leaves that for dead.'

'Is dead, beside *The Ice-cream Bursts*.'

They glared at one another. The woman gulped down her coffee. 'See you round,' she said. Kate got as far as *Call Him* when the door to the Rosella Theatre opened and Sergeant Pryor came out. Rupert went over to him, his skinny tall old body looking as though it were being manipulated by an absent-minded puppet master. 'What's the verdict,' he asked anxiously.

'Oh, far too early to say.'

'You must suspect foul play.'

'There's no real evidence . . .'

'Believe me, Inspector, Bianca Madin wouldn't have killed herself. I *know*.'

'We all find it hard to believe when something like this happens to our friends. But without evidence, and with all these witnesses to the woman's own words . . .'

The old man was weeping now. 'Foul play. I know it was foul play.'

'Come on,' said Kate. 'Let's walk into town. I'll buy you a drink.'

The bar at the Granite was quiet at that time of day. Kate bought two glasses of champagne. 'It's a very healthy drink, champagne,' she said. 'Cheers. To our literary futures.'

She sipped, then added: 'And poor old Bianca. Murdered in the prime of her career.'

'Murdered?'

'Did she fall or was she pushed?'

'You tell me.'

'Oh I don't have to tell you. She was pushed. As you know, since you pushed her.'

Frank burst out laughing. 'Tell me more.'

'Well.' Kate jumped to her feet, slim and energetic in jeans and runners. 'That balustrade. It came up to here on me.' She made a chopping movement with the flat of her hand against her breastbone. 'I'm no giant, but I'm somewhat taller than our Bianca. I tried climbing over that balustrade . . .'

'Ah. You too, the irresistible urge.'

She ignored him. 'I didn't try too hard, in case I succeeded.

219

But I doubt I would've. It'd certainly have been bloody hard work. Bianca never could have done it. Not at twice my age and three times my girth.' Frank looked at her. 'All right. Four times. No. She needed a heave. From a strong young man. You.'

'Oh yes,' said Frank. His eyes gleamed at her. Sardonic. Hastily she went on.

'Why? we hear the jury ask. The literary world is a hotbed of cut-throat competition, but chucking people down twelve storeys on to grand pianos is a new one. Hang on a tick.' She went away and got two more glasses of champagne. 'You can start buying this in a minute.'

'So, dear jury, here is the motive.' She paused for dramatic effect. 'Bianca Madin, who began life as Bertha Mudd, by the way, funny how people like to stick close to their old names when they go pseudonymous, Bianca/Bertha ran a manuscript advisory agency. The Busy B Manuscript Advisory Service and Publishing Agency. Not under either the chosen or the given moniker. Tiny print mentioned a certain Benedict Morrow. Benedict the Blessed, was the message, I reckon. Thirty Years in Publishing, he claimed. Address was a post office box in Leura. Leura is where Bianca Madin lived. Who was also a grateful client. The Busy B gave me my start in the world of books. Providing the essential mixture of enthusiasm and ruthlessness necessary for the writer's development. Etcetera. She offered a variety of plugs. Better than your best friends. The Busy B Agency tells you the truth, and knows how to help you.

'To cut a long story less long—after all, you know all this— hopeful authors sent manuscripts. Correspondence ensued. Not very speedy. The agency didn't claim to be fast. Caring and effective was their style. Lots of detailed not to say finicking suggestions for improvement. Plus contacts. Negotiations with colleagues in the business. Much dangling and tickling. Plenty

of hope. Finally, regret: in the present climate . . . difficult times
. . . but don't despair . . . try us again. A healthy discount for
the second book. And it was cheap to begin with. Seventy dollars.
What a bargain for caring and committed advice. That of course
ought to have been the warning: only the gullible need apply.'

'This is fascinating stuff,' said Frank.

'Then, next thing you know, Bianca Madin's new novel.
Surprise, surprise. Of course it's not yours, not word for word,
not exactly. Quite possibly it's improved. But you recognise it,
don't you, Frank? *The Ice-cream Bursts*, by Frank Downard.'

'Terrible title,' said Frank.

'Doubtless not what you'd have chosen. Of course, I'm
guessing here, about exactly which book is yours, I mean. On
the strength of earlier discussions. But I'm right, aren't I.'

'It's a nice theory. In parts.'

'It explains the amazing creativity of Bianca Madin's work.
Why no two novels were the same. They were all written by
different people. Basically. I wonder how many hopeful writers
she ripped off . . .'

'Okay. Suppose you're right. About the agency ripping off.
How did they get away with it?'

'Young customers. Inexperienced. The delay. The careful
correspondence. By then your book is out under her name.
It's a beginner's word against the doyenne of Oz lit. How could
you prove anything? You've got no power at all. Until one young
man, one Frank Downard, gets jack of it and shoves her over
a balcony. Did you come to the festival with the plan in mind?
Or was it the inspiration of the moment?'

'Do you have any evidence of this? Do you claim you actually
saw it happen?'

'Aha.' Kate laughed. 'You mean was I lurking round the corner?
Did I see you knock on her door, shortly after nine, an ardent

young man, such a fan and so charming, and sexy too, Bianca is fond of a sexy man, especially bearing gifts—you should have been beware, Bianca—and books to sign, and later, leaving lovingly, standing at the door talking, checking that no one observes, not difficult, amazing how you rarely meet anybody in those passages—though maybe not so private as you think— calling her over to the edge she so loves to talk about, offering the dizzy view in some words she can't resist, and . . . adieu Bianca? Would my seeing it make it any more true?'

Frank stood up. 'I think we need another glass of champagne.' Kate watched him go over to the bar. He certainly was rather well built. A neat little bum and long strong arms.

'All right,' he said, when he came back. 'Allow what you say is true. I'm not admitting anything, mind, just for the sake of argument. Two questions. One: how did you work all this out, and two: if you reckon it's true how come you're not telling the sergeant?'

Kate raised her glass. 'That's easy. One answer will do for both your questions. Namely, viz, and to wit: I am the person who wrote *Call Him Soft Names*. Not by that poncy title, I might add. And if you hadn't chucked her over, well, I had some notions in that direction myself.'

Frank began to laugh. 'Salut,' he said, between splutterings, and clinked his glass hard against Kate's. 'I wonder who wrote *Anteroom to a Cage*?' he mused.

Induction

I

*H*ow soft the hot air was today. He could almost believe there were no grating, just the warm soft air like feathers cradling. He lay still, not to disturb it, to hold as long as possible this illusion of perfect warmth; the slightest twitch and the cold would come prying in and he would have to begin the day. His wakings were never luxurious like this; he began to slide back to sleep. He would stay forever in this dream of comfort.

Instinct knew better, dragged him out, jerked his eyes open a nervous crack on tender light. He'd have to go, it was dangerous to stay on the grating after dawn.

Too late. There were people standing about watching him the law no a hospital then he peered through cracked lids craftily

223

to see and not to be seen to see work it out play for time where is the street the grating the cold grey wind who are these people not nurses too fancy doctors then but the room too pretty a bedroom and music but how . . .

He opened his eyes wide lay rigid looked hard at the woman tall red-haired in a white dressing-gown fluffy with swansdown. He'd never seen her before not ever before not even . . . before.

—Where am I, he said, the words furry in his mouth.

—At home, darling, in your very own bed.

—Home . . .

—The apartment . . . the Paris one . . . avenue Foch . . . you'll remember it soon.

The voice offered to soothe with gentle facts. He knew he did not deserve them.

There was another woman blonde in black standing slightly behind the red-haired one. She was distressed and burst into tears quite noisily.

—Whatever . . . does . . . it . . . mean . . .

—Hush, sleep now. Sleep, sleep. You're still not ready to wake. We'll talk all about it later.

It was a bed, not a grating. He could believe that, and it was enough. He slept again. And dreamt of guardian angels, one red-haired in swansdown the other blonde in sinuous black satin all three for he was there too enskied on floating clouds of soft warm air. A disturbing dream, indeed violating. He did not believe in heaven, certainly not with houris.

II

They'd spent a lot of time finding him, going out late, after two o'clock when the clochards settled down in their chosen warm places for the last peaceful hours of the night. Bending

224

over lumpy sleeping bodies layered with newspapers, shining a bright torch into ruined faces, getting cuffed at and cursed, called foul names, clutched at and breathed on with putrid breaths, murmuring apologies, they were looking for a friend, until Muriel said, this is the one. They were on the Quai St Bernard, not far from the Pont d'Austerlitz, where the wind blows chill off the river. He was curled into a foetal comma, and his face for all its stubble and dirt and inflamed cheeks had a slight vulnerable calm. But more important than that, he was too far gone into unconsciousness to wake up when handled. They turned him, not gently, to see.

— My uncle, said Muriel to his companion on the grating, who had woken up. The two men had lain together like bedmates, an explanation seemed politic. She bent over him. The warm dry exhausted breath of the metro wafted up into her face. Warm indeed, but dead, dead.

— We've been looking for him for weeks. He gets away like this every now and then, said Jean-Claude embroidering.

The car came up. Marcus brought a blanket. They loaded him into it and carried him away. A perfect stranger whom none of them had ever seen before.

III

Whose hands had he fallen into?

Dramatis personae

Muriel   Half-French, half-American, twice rich. Tall and red-haired. Not pretty, but able to buy the expertise to appear so.

Jean-Claude   A doctor, defrocked, with a fondness for cocaine.

Treated Muriel's second husband in his clinic for fashionable alcoholics, when still able to practise.

Marcus   Muriel's bodyguard. Hired when there was a spate of kidnappings in the avenue Foch. Young and handsome, good at doing all sorts of more amusing things with bodies than guarding them. He drives the cars too. Slumming in low-class cafes with him gave her the idea in the first place.

Anice   Lady-in-waiting. Thin, brittle, with silver-gilt curls. A brief filmstar hampered now her looks are tarnishing by inability to act. Had an affair with Muriel when latter's third marriage ended and she decided to give up men. Both found Lesbos a nice place to visit but don't want to live there.

Sundry servants   Butler cook parlourmaid. Most underworked.

And who is he? For the nonce:

The clochard   Can be translated as beggar, vagabond, tramp, bum. Extremely dirty and smelly.

Thus the characters. Now for the settings:

a. a cold and windy street by the river

b. an apartment on the avenue Foch. A number of big rooms with immense vertical space and very high windows and mirrors over fireplaces to match. Designed for grand people, whose emotions passions or perhaps philosophies needed a lot of room to expand in.

IV

They didn't try to shave him, but washed him several times carefully with fine soap, and powdered him, rubbed cream into his sad chapped face—that metro air is hideously drying, said Anice—dressed him in a long lawn nightshirt and put him to bed, propped on frilled feather pillows and covered with a duvet although the central heating kept the apartment summer warm.

He didn't wake up all through this because Jean-Claude who still had contacts had given him an injection; in his alcoholics clinic he'd been skilled at engineering belated gentle awakenings.

They threw away all his clothes but kept his papers.

V

Muriel liked being rich there were so many good things clothes and food and places to go and beautiful objects furniture carpets paintings old porcelain and houses castles ranches villas by the sea. But things, things above all things, it was not possible to go on endlessly acquiring things, buy a château buy a painting the thrill was the same and increasingly briefer finally boring. Yet for a rich person it was hard to know what else to do.

She was educated, well enough, and talented, to a degree; could have earned a living in a number of ways. But wealthy leisure was another matter.

The arts, of course. Theatre cinema ballet opera. But for the spectator art is short and life is long.

Good works, perhaps. But that was money too charity buying a sense of virtue. Marriage had failed thrice and children were fearful. And love had become simply its gratification and a pastime but a short-lived one; there was more time than love could pass in the life of a rich woman of thirty-six.

So then there was power. Fashionable notion. Everybody wanted it. Husbands and wives, lovers and mistresses, parents and children. Teachers and bosses and dress designers. Doctors

and truck-drivers and politicians. All playing little gods or big
ones. God-frogs in vari-sized pools. Like Muriel in this small
puddle of the weak and silly and wicked and bored, all prepared
for moral or monetary or no good reason to follow the dictates
of her will.

See her having fun, exercising it.

So she told the clochard that he was Christophe Matois
and her lost husband whom she had tearfully sought in all the
streets of Paris, and now she had found him again would nurse
back to health and cheer. Whose memory she would lovingly
reconstruct for him if he couldn't do it himself. Her butler brought
him delicate nourishing soups in which were concentrated all
the cook's art, the doctor—so Jean-Claude was presented—gave
the occasional injection to tickle his memory glands said the
ghost of his professional manner, and Muriel devoted wife sat
on the bed and proffered him enticing morsels of their past
bliss.

VI

Christophe Matois. Horrible name. How he must have been
teased at school. Sly boots. Sly fox, Christopher Crafty. Perhaps
that had been the start of it all the illness the mind cracking
under the weight of it, making another life another name opting
out remembering nothing. Or nothing that was real, apparently.
He could have sworn he was Pierre Chabrier a plain name
no judgements to get at you and fancy it a whole plain career
to go with it. The decent law practice the failure the embezzlement
the gaol the drinking the gratings . . .

Amazing how real it all seemed. It sat in his brain like fact.
Amazing the power of the mind. Construct a whole career. Fill
it with painful details, sickening details needing drunkenness

to bear. And suppress a whole other life: his marriage to this beautiful loving creature in all the pleasant places of Europe and America too which he had thought he had never set foot in, and he believing himself a bachelor with an old proud mother dying of grief when her clever son with heart-breaking publicity was tried and sent to gaol.

Amazing what the mind can believe. When the reality here in this grand apartment in the avenue Foch with its ceilings so high you could suppose the air rarefied up there and its huge feathery bed visited now that his convalescence allowed by a beautiful loving wife sexier than he had remembered women could be—how could he have forgotten that—was hardly a cross to bear. He would try to remember to talk to that psychologist. There was probably a fancy medical name for his condition, for a man completely forgetting a good life and constructing a horrific one in its place.

He hardly ever had any injections now, just the pills. He spent part of each day up, dressed in scented soft clothes smooth against his skin, taking little walks in the apartment though he was tired by the least exertion, talking to Anice his wife's dear friend who'd been bridesmaid at their wedding and could still summon up a tear if not a photograph to celebrate, the treat of the day lunch with Muriel, delicate dishes served on a small table in the great window of the dining-room that overlooked the avenue, watching through the web of leafless branches the traffic moving endlessly in the wide street below. Looking across at the ornamented building on the other side great rooms high windows the mirror image of their own and marvelling that his memory should fail to function despite the care of this doting stranger-wife, greedy for all the details of the derelict's life, saying talk it out my darling, and then we'll understand.

VII

— It's all great fun, Muriel, but it'll pall soon, said Jean-Claude. Then what on earth are you going to do with him? He waved the small silver spoon he used for his cocaine. Typical elaborate gesture.

— You could marry him, said Anice. You're about due for another go.

It was not at all possible to tell whether Anice's remarks were made from malice or unintelligence. But the charm of that was short-lived, and Muriel had come close to the end of it.

— I might at that, she said. I might retire to the country and raise children. He dotes on me, you know.

— My dear, is marital bliss really your scene, said Jean-Claude. He picked his nails with the spoon's chased handle.

— I can't tell till I've tried, can I. Fourth time lucky, perhaps.

— Sit on his knee and feed him little tit-bits of his pseudo-memory. Popping them into his mouth with little pursed fingers . . . It's a dream of romance.

— Well, can I have Marcus, if you're getting married, asked Anice.

— Darling, do you think you can afford him, said Muriel.

— On the other hand, she went on, I might put him back where I found him, on the grating in the Quai St Bernard dead drunk, and when he wakes up he'll believe it all a dream, the most vivid dream anybody ever had.

— Oh, superb, said Jean-Claude. The perfect ending, the poetic ending. Oh indeed. You my darling are the most brilliant woman in the world.

He came across the room and kissed her hand. She looked at him coldly.

— Yes. I know.

She stood up. The folds of her Yves St Laurent skirt, quantities of fawn suede, fell opulently round her knees.

— There's a third possibility, which neither of you have thought of, she sneered at them. I might tell him all about it, let him into the joke, and see what happens. Go easy on the valium for a bit, so his mind's working, then tell him. Should be interesting. I think he's got quite a good mind. I'm sick of dumb people, beautiful dumb people are a pain in the neck.

She frowned at Anice, and would have at Marcus had he been there. Jean-Claude said,

— Well, of course it's a possibility. Perhaps the most titillating one. Doesn't have the pure poetry of the last, but does have the conflict of drama.

Muriel looked at him with distaste too. She thought I am tired of this man compulsively verbalising my life. It's a mental tic.

She thought of Christophe Matois. Not yet with distaste. Marry him; abandon him; enlighten him. She couldn't decide yet. Which was a good thing, of course. The most amusing part of the whole game could be deciding on a fate for him.

Life is long, art is short. But less so when its matter is life. Muriel the painter, Christophe the canvas. Muriel the writer, Christophe the story. Oh yes, there was much still to tell.

Marion Halligan
Lovers' Knots

If your house was burning down, what would you save? The money, the silver, the compact disc collection? The original Dali print? The last plate from your great-grandmother's dinner set? Standing like a spectator on the lawn, hearing the greedy eating of the flames at your possessions, smelling the noisome smoke of your belongings, suddenly you disobey. You bunch up your skirt or your shirt in a mask against the heat and run inside like a footballer ducking detaining hands, to save your precious . . . what?

The boxes of photographs . . .

From Ada the matriarch to Eva the waif, from gentle Alice to sharp-eyed Sebastian . . . a family saga reduced to the shapely form of its best stories. A novel about ways of seeing and means of living . . .

The much acclaimed writer Marion Halligan has written a brilliant evocation of life in Australia. The stories swapped between generations fill this large novel with passion and sorrow.

Marion Halligan's writing is as shining with life as the rivers that flow through these pages. The style is as polished as the amber its women wear and the story as full of pictures as the files of the photographer Mikelis who needs his camera to see the world.

Lovers' Knots is one of the year's finest novels.

'. . . crackling with life and mortality . . . Halligan's magical word pictures have that serene intensity that is now her hallmark.'

Robert Dessaix

Minerva rrp $14.95
ISBN 1 86330 158 3

Thea Astley

Vanishing Points

I feel I am a lot more warmable to than Clifford. Clifford is my husband. Well, that's a misuse of a term as well. There's nothing husbanding about Clifford, even though we are legally tied. (That word should be spelt with an 'r'.) . . .

Thea Astley, Australia's most acclaimed and awarded writer, presents two novellas which sweep the reader on sentimental journeys towards an ending rather than a beginning.

Julie Truscott, a seemingly ordinary housewife, and Macintosh Hope, a disenchanted academic, each flee from lives they cannot control. The balance of their flight is destroyed by Clifford Truscott – Julie's real estate husband and the rapacious developer of Mac's neighbouring island.

In *Vanishing Points* Thea Astley is at her best.

'. . . an ebullient wit and unflagging comic energy.'

Helen Daniel, the Age

Minerva rrp $14.95 pb
ISBN 1 86330 186 0

Rosie Scott

Feral City

It was a dangerous [time] . . . I was suddenly and irretrievably in the presence of the past, Lin's old car, blue foxgloves in bloom by the rushing white-bouldered rivers, a long trip we made once through the light-filled landscapes of the south . . . At the moment of seeing all this I became blind and deaf to everything else. It was the first time since I'd come to the city that I'd allowed myself to taste that sort of memory. Never mind that I was roaring down an unknown road loaded with the tools of a new trade, concoms and soup, clean syringes, on a mercy run to bring in lost city souls from the dead . . .

Feral City is the city of our future, its centre a wasteland peopled by addicts, violent gangs and the homeless. In a gesture of defiant optimism, two sisters – one a warrior, the other a survivor – open a bookshop in the heart of this decaying city. Their bizarre and moving story mirrors the fragile balance between defeat and courage.

With the passionate imagination we now expect from her, Rosie Scott presents a future shock which is alive with imminent danger.

'At its best, Rosie Scott's writing is reminiscent of the work of Colombian genius Grabriel Garcia Marquez.'

Ken Spillman, the *West Australian*

Minerva rrp $14.95 pb
ISBN 1 86330 182 8

Susan Johnson

Flying Lessons

In the early 1920s in a small town in north Queensland, Emma
James, daughter of an Anglican family, disobeyed her bigoted father's
wishes and married Sam Lubrano – a Catholic and son of an Italian
immigrant.

And so begins a story of the heart.

In the 1980s Ria Lubrano, singer of advertising jingles, leaves
Sydney without a trace, journeying to the tableland town in search of
her missing brother, her roots and herself. She believes there is a
meaning in the past that will bring purpose to her life if she can but
reach back across time.

Through Emma's and Ria's stories, Susan Johnson weaves a
moving saga of family life and the passions that pattern our identity.

'. . . a knowing and feeling author whose text sweeps along,
intriguing and engaging the readers . . . [Susan Johnson] writes of
her own context with such appealing strength and . . . searching
critique . . .'

Stephen Knight, the *Sydney Morning Herald*

Minerva rrp $14.95 pb
ISBN 1 86330 078 3

Susan Johnson

Flying Lessons

In the early 1920s in a small town in north Queensland, Emma-Jane, daughter of an Anglican family, disobeyed her bigoted father, a widower, and married Sam Lubrano – a Catholic and son of an Italian immigrant.

And so begins a story of the future.

In the 1990s Ria Lubrano, singer of advertising jingles, leaves Sydney without a trace, journeying to the Queensland town in search of her missing brother. Her roots and herself. She believes there is a meaning in the past that will bring purpose to her life, if she can but reach back across time.

Through Emma's and Ria's stories, Susan Johnson weaves a moving saga of family life and the passions that pattern our identity

'a knowing and feeling author whose text sweeps along ... invigorating and engaging the readers.' ... 'Susan Johnson writes of her own context with such appealing strength and ... searching empathy.'

Stephen Knight, the Sydney Morning Herald

Minerva rrp $11.95 pb
ISBN 1 86330 078 0